Also by Kristin Hunter

THE SOUL BROTHERS AND SISTER LOU

BOSS CAT

GUESTS IN THE
PROMISED LAND

GUESTS IN THE PROMISED LAND

Stories by
Kristin Hunter

CHARLES SCRIBNER'S SONS
NEW YORK

J
H

Printed in the United States of America
Library of Congress Catalog Card Number 72-9036
SBN 684-13227-3 (Cloth)

For my daughter-by-marriage

Mona Lattany

with love

CONTENTS

GUESTS IN THE PROMISED LAND

Hero's Return

I tell you, I was about to explode, I was so excited when I heard my big brother Junior was coming home.

Junior spent eighteen months in the House. He took out a long stretch, cause somebody shot off a gun the day Junior and his corner boys held up the Kravitz's ice-cream store. Nobody got hurt, but Mrs. Kravitz hollered like somebody had killed her. The others got away, and Junior caught the whole blame. It was enough to put him away for a long, long time.

My corner boys were real impressed when I told them. Course they acted like it wasn't nothing, like any one of them could do eighteen months standing on his head. But they were impressed right on, and jealous besides, not having a brother like Junior or anybody else famous in the family.

I remember the headline—"Aging Couple Robbed" —and Junior's picture in the paper. I cut it out and saved it. It's still in my snapshot album that I never did put any other pictures in cause I never got the camera.

My brother was big stuff. Front-page stuff. And now he was coming home.

Josh he acted like it weren't nothing. "Eighteen months?" he said. "What's that? I hear you get your own TV in the House, and your own room."

No ghetto kid has his own room, except me after Junior went away. And now he was coming home, and me glad to share it with him again.

"Yeah," says Marquis, "I hear tell they have ice cream every night up there. Double scoops on Sundays. And people come around and give them cigarettes, things like that."

We only used to get ice cream when we found enough soda bottles to return to the store. And now they got those No Deposit No Return bottles, we don't hardly ever get none unless somebody's Mom gives him a dime. If she does, you got to run all the way home to eat it by yourself, else fight some bigger kids for it. And even if you get past the big guys, there's *your* boys, Josh and Duke and Leroy and Marquis, all wanting to take turns licking off your ice-cream cone.

"Man, I ain't studying no ice cream," said Leroy. He acts like he's the baddest thing on McCarter Street just cause he's thirteen and the rest of us is only twelve. "I could use some cigarettes, though."

This was one time I was with Leroy. I don't think about ice cream much no more cause I don't like to go in Kravitz's store since it happened. I favor my brother in the face, and old Mrs. Kravitz might start yelling her head off again. You can get cigarettes anywhere.

But we don't never have enough money, unless King or one of the other big-time hustlers on the corner gives us some to run an errand. The other hustlers only give us fifty cents, but sometimes King gives a whole dollar. I seen him take a roll of money thick as my fist out of his pocket plenty of times.

We were standing around that July morning, waiting for King to show up, hoping he would give one of us something to do. We all want to be hustlers when we grow up. A hustler is somebody who lives by his wits, you might say, and King was the king of them all.

It was hot enough to boil water on the sidewalk that morning, and my foot was blistered from a hole in my sneaks. I was thinking, Maybe when Junior gets home he'll pull off another job and get me a new pair, when King glides up to the curb in his white air-conditioned Hog.

The Cadillac was about half a block long, and a sharp fox in a blonde wig was sitting beside King. He looked cool as an ice cube in there, his wavy hair shining and diamonds flashing on his hands.

"Hey, you boy. Come here!" He flicked a little button in the Hog, and the window slid down easy as greased silk. Josh and Duke and Leroy and Marquis all hit the sidewalk, but I had a head start in my sneakers, hole and all. I got to the car a full three feet ahead of them.

Then—man!—King shoved the girl out of the car and held open the door for *me*. I hopped in and closed the door, and we eased away from the curb. Leroy and Josh and Duke and Marquis were left standin' there with their mouths hangin' open.

"Have a cigarette, kid," King said, and handed me a pack of Marlboros with the top flipped up. But what was inside didn't look like no Marlboros. The paper was pink and it had been rolled by hand.

King handed me the dashboard lighter. I lit up and held the smoke in.

King lit a real Marlboro and leaned back, steering the Hog through tight traffic with one hand. "Kid," he said, "you got to the car first, so you must be the most ambitious one on the corner. You want to get ahead in this world?"

I nodded. I couldn't speak cause the smoke had me all choked up inside.

"Well," King said, "how'd you like to be my right-hand man?"

"Yes!" I cried.

"All you got to do," King said, "is pass this stuff out among the kids." And he pulls a plastic bag out from under the seat. "When they want more, you come back to me. I'll tell you what to charge 'em."

And then King pulled that big old wad out of his pocket and plucked off a crisp new five and handed it to me. My eyes popped. But I didn't lose my cool. Just sat back and inhaled that pink cigarette like a man.

It was making me feel like a man too. Like I could do anything. I put the five in the pocket of my jeans and sucked in the smoke and held it in like I seen Leroy do one time. I felt ten feet tall, higher than high. Way above the funky scuffling people we were cruising by on Madison.

"Man," I said to King, "this is some good stuff."

"Oughta be. It came all the way from Panama," King said. "Listen, kid. The cops don't exactly dig this action, you understand?"

"I'm hip," I said.

"Don't let any of 'em catch you with it. And don't smoke it all yourself, neither."

"Don't worry, King. I'll take care of business," I told him.

"Good," King said and grinned. The wrinkles in his handsome face sank in and made it look like a skull. "You were the one I wanted, kid, you know that? I just didn't know your name."

That made me feel good, but at the same time I got a funny feeling in the stomach. Like when I've had some corn chips and a cherry soda and Mom puts a big platter on the table and I can't eat.

King was waving at people and honking his horn. Everybody stopped what they were doing and waved back. King's the biggest man in town. Everybody wants to know him. And there *I* was, riding right beside him.

Then we turned sharp into McCarter, and there on the corner was Junior. Thinner than when I saw him last, and with dark smudges under his eyes. But he was *home*.

"I got to get out now, King," I said. "That's my brother over there." Junior looked up and saw me.

"Jody!" he cried and took a step toward me. I had meant to shake hands, the way men do, but instead I flew at him and we hugged right there on the street. My head used to just hit the middle of his chest, but now it touched his chin.

We stepped back, kind of embarrassed, and shook hands like I had meant to do in the first place.

"Boy," he said, "you must've grown a foot. Keep it up, you be tall as me."

And he laughed and rubbed my head. But his eyes were all squinched up like he was trying to keep tears back. I didn't like to see him looking like that, so I started talking fast.

"Did they treat you all right at the House, Junior? I bet you made 'em respect you. I bet they knew you weren't no one to mess with. Didn't they, Junior?"

"I don't want to talk about it," he said. "What were you doing in that car?"

The big Hog with the special-made front license plate, *K I N G*, was still parked at the corner.

"Tell you later," I said, though I was busting to tell him then. "I want to hear how you made out in the slammer."

"Let's get home," he said. But before we could, Duke and Leroy and Josh and Marquis came running up. They surrounded us and pelted Junior with questions.

"Did they give you a TV, man?"

"How was the food? Good?"

"Who'd you meet in there? Any of the big cats?"

"Yeah, I bet you got connections now. I bet you ready for the big time."

Them guys. Sometimes I wish they would leave a guy alone. But they my boys, and they was as excited to see him as I was.

Junior just kept steady walkin', his mouth set in a tight line, saying nothing to the guys until they gave up and fell back. We got to our building. And there over the door was a big cardboard sign Mom had lettered in crayon: WELCOME HOME SON. Just like they do for the heroes that come back from Vietnam.

Junior stood and stared at the sign for a minute. Then he stepped over the kids that are always hanging around out front and yanked the sign down. He ripped it in four pieces and dropped it in the gutter.

"Junior!" I hollered. "What you want to do that for? You'll make Mom feel bad."

"I already made her feel bad," he said. "Come on." He pushed me ahead of him into the hallway.

"You didn't even speak to nobody," I complained. "Josh and Leroy and them, and your old ace Tom Cat, and old Mr. Baltimore. And Mrs. Walters. She was sittin' in the front window like always. You didn't even speak to *her*. They all want to see you, Junior. They been askin' about you while you been away."

"I spoke to *you*, didn't I?" he said. "Which door is it?"

Our building has so many apartments in it I lost count. Still, it was kind of a shock that Junior didn't remember his own apartment door. Made me realize how long he'd been away. And how far, even though you can reach the House by the number 14 bus.

"One more flight up," I told him. When we got there I didn't have to give him any more directions.

Mom was standing in the door with her arms held out in welcome. Junior tried to push past her and get inside, but she had to give him a hug and have her a cry right there. People from the other apartments were watching. I was embarrassed, so I pushed between Mom and Junior and got through the door. That separated them.

Mom stepped back into the apartment. Junior followed her and shut the door real quick behind him. He locked all the locks, the bolt and the chain lock and the police lock that goes right down into the floor. Like he didn't want to ever let anybody in again.

"Lord, child, let me look at you," Mom said when she had dried her eyes on her apron. "Looks like you didn't hardly get enough to eat in that place."

That bothered me some, to tell you the truth. It wasn't at all like what Leroy and them had been saying. But maybe it was just that Junior had lost all his baby fat and was getting lean and hard.

He stood there in the middle of the floor like he hadn't really come to stay and was planning to leave any second. It kept Mom from fussing over him anymore. She started fussing over the stove instead, measuring rice and stirring the chicken and okra. Man! It sure smelled delicious. Suddenly I was real hungry.

"Stewed chicken and okra tonight, honey," she said to

Junior. "Your favorite supper. And later I got some people coming in who want to see my son."

"I don't want to see any people," Junior said. "I'm kind of tired. I'm going to take me a little rest."

And without another word he went into our room and shut the door.

"Anything you say, son," Mom said. But he didn't hear her. He had already slammed the bedroom door.

Pretty soon she started crying again. I couldn't stand that, so I took a beer out of the ice box and went to the room and knocked.

"Is that you, Jody?"

"Yes."

"Come in."

"I thought you might like a beer," I said, shutting the door behind me.

"Thanks," he said and took it. He didn't say any more, just lay on his back on his bed, staring at the ceiling. I sat on the edge of my bed and watched him for a while. The room was getting tenser by the minute.

"Planning a job, huh?" I finally said.

"I can't get a job. I've got a record."

"I mean a *big-time* job," I said. "Like you pulled off at Kravitz's, only bigger."

He rolled over and looked at me for the first time. "You think I'm a hero, don't you?" he said. "A big-shot crook. Like in the movies."

"Sure, Junior," I said eagerly. "All the guys do. They expect you to do great things. You got the connections and the smarts now. You must know a lot more than when you went in the House. You was only seventeen then. Now you're a man."

"Yeah, I'm a man," Junior said disgustedly, "and ain't a thing in this town I can do. Nobody's going to hire a jail-bird."

"It's all right," I said. "I can take care of us for a while, till you get yourself together."

I pulled out the five and showed it to him.

He was up on his feet, standing over me. "Where'd you get that?"

Something in his manner scared me, but I went on. "King gave it to me. And I'm going to make a lot more. Selling this." I pulled the plastic bag out of my pocket. "It's—"

"I know what it is," Junior said and took off his belt. "Go flush it down the toilet."

"But, Junior—"

He gave me a whack with the back of his hand. It caught me by surprise and sent me sprawling on the floor.

"Flush it, I said. And come right back here when you finished."

I trembled, cause I knew what was coming. He had the belt in his hand, folded over double. My face was stinging from the whack, and I was beginning to cry, more from surprise than anything else. But on my way to the bathroom and back I didn't let Mom see me.

Junior was waiting for me when I got back. "So you want to go to jail, huh? All right, I'll show you what jail is like."

He locked the door from the inside and gave me the worst whipping I ever had in my life. The only one, in fact. Pop left home before I was born, and Mom was always too kindhearted to beat us.   KIM

She had heard me yelling and was at the door, banging on it to be let in. "Junior, what's going on in there? What you doing to my baby?"

"Saving him, that's what," Junior yelled back through the door. "If he ain't already ruint."

He didn't open the door, either. He went right on whipping me. When he was through, he said, "You going to stay away from that slick hustler, huh? You going to stay off that corner and leave those pint-size hoods alone?"

I didn't answer, I was so mad.

"All right. You got a week to think about it." He shut the door behind him and locked me in.

"What you doing to my baby?" Mom cried again.

Junior said, "He wants to go to jail. So let him try it for a few days. Let him live on bread and water and stay in solitary and get knocked around every time he opens his mouth."

Mom let out a wail that sounded like a police siren, but it didn't change Junior's mind. He brought me bread and water for supper and took out the mattresses so he could sleep on them in the front room. *I* would sleep on the springs and get a taste of what a prison bed was like.

He explained it all to me patiently, like he wasn't angry anymore. "The small-time crooks, they get to talk to each other. But the real big-time criminals like you get solitary.

And if they *real* bad actors, the guards take the springs out of the cell too. Then they sleep on the floor. I'm your guard. And if you a bad actor, I get to knock you around. Understand?"

But that was all he would say. Once or twice he knocked me around a little, just to show me it wasn't a game. The rest of the time, he didn't say or do nothing. Just brought the bread and water and took me to the bathroom.

I got so lonesome in there I wished he would come in, even to beat me. The old bedsprings stuck me no matter which way I turned, so I lay on the floor, thinking about stewed chicken and okra and having cramps in my belly. All I had to listen to was their arguments.

"You gonna kill him," Mom said.

"No," Junior told her. "He might get killed in jail. That happens to lots of guys. But this way he's gonna live."

"He's only a baby," she wailed.

"He's big enough to get in big trouble. I got home just in time."

The first night wasn't so bad. I expected Mom to come to my rescue any minute. But he wouldn't let her. In the morning I heard her going off to work. They would fire her if she took off two days in a row, so she had to go.

The second and third days, I lay there trying to remember boss things I'd done with the guys, like chasing girls in the park and stealing fruit and sneaking rides on the back of trucks. But pretty soon those things bored me too.

On the fourth day, I got some of my school books down from the closet and began reading. I even got interested in history.

Junior came in while I was lying on my stomach with the book open on the floor in front of me. For a scary moment I thought he was going to take it away. But he just looked at me. And then he smiled.

"Gonna be a big-time criminal like me?"

"No."

"Gonna drop out of school like I did?"

"No." I paused and thought very carefully, then surprised myself by what I said. "I think I might go to that tutoring place at Mom's church and make up math. I think I could pass it this time."

"What I think," Junior said, "is you ready to come out now. I'm gonna parole you. But you got to watch your step, you hear? No associating with known criminals. No messing up. A single slip, and back you go."

Then he fixed me a big breakfast. He explained that since we didn't have a father anymore, he had to be the man of the house. It made him feel good, he said, knowing at least part of what he had to do.

Then he let me go out on the street.

It looked different, like a place I hadn't seen in years and years. With all the slick people and crooks and hustlers, it looked like a place where I didn't want to stay very long.

"Hey, man," Leroy hollered at me, "where you been?"

I was still weak and wobbly in spite of the breakfast. But I felt stronger and older than Leroy and the others. I knew things they still had to learn. One thing I knew was if I ever made it off that corner, I would have to make it alone.

"I been," I said, "in jail."

Then I left them and went on my way, knowing where I was going and walking like a man.

BeeGee's Ghost

It's my own fault, what happened to my dog BeeGee. I shouldn't have bragged on her so much. But that Leroy Lawson was talking so smart I had to do something.

We was in my front yard on Highway 95, tossing sticks for BeeGee to fetch. I said, "BeeGee is about the smartest dog in South Carolina, I betcha. Maybe she's even the smartest dog in the whole U.S.A."

Leroy said, "Huh! My hounddog Jake is smarter. He knows how to hunt rabbits and coons."

"Yeah," I said, "but that's *all* he knows. BeeGee knows about a hundred tricks. She'll fetch anything I tell her to." I picked up a ball. "Even if I throw this ball way across the highway in them woods, she'll find it and bring it back."

Leroy said, "You better not, Freddy. She might run in front of them cars."

I should have listened. The cars go by our house all day and night like machine-gun bullets. *Zip! Zam! Zoom!*

But I paid Leroy no mind. "Not BeeGee," I said.

"That dumb hound of *yours* might run in front of a car, but *my* dog's too smart. C'mon, BeeGee. Fetch!"

And I threw the ball. BeeGee took off across the highway like a streak of white lightning.

She almost made it. But an Oldsmobile came around the curve doing eighty, and he couldn't stop in time. The man came across the highway carrying BeeGee's body.

My Grandma came out of the house all ready to scold me. "Lord, Freddy, did you let that dog run out on the highway?"

"Yes, it's my fault," I said.

When Grandma saw me crying, she softened up and turned on the Oldsmobile driver instead. "Well, what do you people expect? Runnin' highways past people's front doors and breakin' the speed limit. A wonder it wasn't my grandson."

Grandma can be pretty rough when she's mad. That white man drove off in a hurry.

"Don't grieve, Freddy," Grandma said. "Everybody's got to go sometime. The main thing is to give her a nice funeral."

"A funeral? Just like a person?" Leroy asked.

"Well, she was *almost* a person," Grandma said. "She was Freddy's best friend, except for you. And she's got to have a proper burial. If a person ain't laid to rest in the ground by their family, they become a ghost. And their spirit walks the earth forever."

"Gosh." Leroy was scared, I could tell. As for me, I didn't know what to think. I had never heard of a ghost dog before, but we got all other kinds of hants down here, so why not? I mean, if there can be demons, witches, and spirits, why not ghost animals?

But I didn't know where to bury BeeGee.

"Do they have cemeteries for pets, just like for people?" I asked.

"Sure!" Leroy said. "There's a big one over near Florence. I seen it the last time we drove over there to go shopping."

Grandma seemed upset. "Hush your fool mouth, Leroy. You don't know what you're talking about."

But I had been there too, and I remembered the place. "No, he's right, Grandma!" I cried. "I know where it is. That's where we're gonna take BeeGee. She was the best dog in the U.S.A., and I want her to have a nice grave."

Grandma wasn't too happy about our plans. But she helped us put BeeGee in a laundry basket and cover her up with an old blanket.

We started off, Leroy and me each holding one handle. The basket got pretty heavy after we'd gone about two miles. But we made it to the pet cemetery.

It seemed like a nice place. It had pretty green lawns and little white headstones, just like a high-class cemetery for people.

Leroy and I went inside the office. The man behind the desk growled, "What do you boys want?" He wasn't very friendly.

But I spoke right up. "We want to arrange a funeral for a dog."

The man acted like he didn't want to wait on us. But finally he put a piece of paper in his typewriter. "Age of dog?"

"Seven years old," I said.

"Sex of dog?"

"She was a lady dog."

"OK, female. Race of dog?"

That one really stopped me. Then I said, "White, I guess. She was a white dog." Because BeeGee was almost pure Spitz and white as snow.

"Owner of dog?"

"Me. Frederick Douglass Jackson."

The man jumped up. "This is *your* dog? You want to bury *your* dog here?"

"That's right," I said.

"Well, I'm sorry. I thought she belonged to someone else. We don't take colored dogs."

Leroy decided to argue. "But he told you she was white." He pulled back the blanket. "Look. White all over."

The man took a look. "She's white, all right," he admitted. He seemed sort of confused.

At last he said, "You'll have to take it up with the boss. All I do is fill out the forms around here." He sighed. "All right, let's get on with it. Name of dog?"

"BeeGee," I said. "It stands for Brown Girl."

"*What?*"

When I think about it now, the expression on that man's face was really comical. But it didn't seem funny then.

I explained that BeeGee was BeeGee the Second. She was named for the first dog I had, a brown police dog.

"That settles it," the man said. He tore up the form angrily. "With a name like that, we can't take her here. You'll have to take her to a cemetery for colored dogs." He pointed to the door.

Leroy and I knew we were licked. But we didn't know what to do next. There ain't no such thing as a pet cemetery for black people, at least not down our way. Poor as our folks are, it's all they can do to buy ground to bury each other in.

It was dark when we got outside. Felt like a rainstorm was blowing up. The wind was crying in the pine trees. *Whoo—Whoo.* And Leroy's eyes were big and white and scared.

"Freddy," he said, "you think what your Grandma said is true? About BeeGee becoming a ghost if she ain't buried?"

"I don't know."

"Well," Leroy said, "I ain't waiting to find out. I just remembered my Mom's looking for me."

And he took off down the road like a ghost was already chasing him.

I wasn't scared like Leroy. I was just mad cause he left me. But I couldn't carry that basket by myself. I got about fifteen steps with it, then had to leave it under a pine tree.

When I got home, Grandma didn't ask me what had happened, and I didn't tell her. I just sat down at the table and helped myself to her good yams and fried chicken and succotash.

While we were eating, the storm really hit. The wind howled, and the rain beat against the windows like BB shot. I was having my second dish of potato poon for dessert when I heard the noise at the door.

"What's that, Freddy?" Grandma asked.

"Must be the storm, Grandma," I said.

"Well," she said, "maybe my hearing's going bad. I thought I heard a scratching at that door. But I must have been wrong. Guess I better go upstairs and make sure all the windows are shut."

When she was gone, I heard it again. A scratching and a low whine, like BeeGee used to make when she wanted to get in.

Without even thinking, I got up out of habit and opened the back door. There was nothing there.

But a few seconds later, I got sprayed. Just as if a dog was standing in the room and shaking itself all over to get dry!

I was too worried about what Granny would say to be scared. "Over here, girl," I said and pointed to the corner. "Lie down."

What happened next was really spooky! There was nobody but me in the room. But a trail of muddy paw prints appeared, leading from the door to the corner.

My skin began to tingle with fear. But I got the mop. I had just mopped up the last of the paw prints when Grandma came back.

"Why is this floor wet?" she wanted to know.

"Uh . . . I spilled some milk," I said.

"I smell wet dog," she said next. "There's a dog in this room."

"I don't smell anything, Grandma," I lied. But I should have known better than to think I could fool her.

She got up to make herself a cup of tea. To get the tea canister, she had to go to the cupboard in the corner. When she did, there was a loud yelp of pain.

"You stepped on BeeGee's foot!" I cried.

Grandma whirled. "Frederick Douglass Jackson, you ain't told me what happened today. Did those folks at the cemetery chase you away?"

"Yes, Grandma. They said they didn't take colored dogs."

"Uh-huh. I could've told you that would happen. Some folks are so mean and low they even prejudiced against animals. She ain't buried yet?"

"No," I said. "I didn't know where to take her. Besides, Leroy ran off, and I couldn't carry her by myself."

"Well, she followed you home."

There was no point in denying it. Grandma is the biggest expert on hants in Florence County. Besides, we could both hear BeeGee's tail thumping the floor.

"I got to send her away." Grandma shook some yellow powder out of a can into a dish. "Sulphur," she said. Ghosts can't stand burning sulphur." She set the powder on fire. Then she lit a yellow candle with the same match and sat there staring into the flame.

Pretty soon, a pitiful whining started up in the corner. Then the paw prints appeared, crisscrossing all over the linoleum.

I didn't like being haunted by BeeGee's ghost. But I couldn't stand the way she was suffering. "Grandma, please stop," I begged.

"I can't spend the night under this roof with a ghost," she said. "Even if it's just an animal ghost."

The whining became a howl.

"If you don't stop," I said, "I'll leave the house *with* her." And I blew out the candle.

Grandma looked mad enough to hit me. But all she said was, "You got a better idea?"

"Let her stay till morning. Then we'll ask Reverend Boggs to bury her in the churchyard."

Grandma was against it. That was the family plot, where *she* intended to be buried. She had saved up for a nice funeral. She had already bought her dress and her coffin. And she wasn't about to share her last resting place with a dog.

"It's against the natural order of things," she said.

But I went on pleading for BeeGee. "She won't take up much room," I said. I was crying. "You *said* she was almost a person, Grandma."

When Grandma saw me crying, she gave in. "But I won't go to sleep tonight," she said, pointing to the corner. "Not with *that* in here."

So she sat up all night in the kitchen. I did too.

Reverend Boggs wouldn't give us permission to bury

BeeGee in our plot at Grace Baptist, though. So we buried her in our backyard. Leroy brought a wooden crate
for the coffin. Grandma brought flowers. And I preached
the sermon: "Lord, you know she was a good dog. Take
care of her. Amen."

From that time on, we had peace in the house.

But I'll never forget the night we spent with BeeGee's
ghost in the kitchen.

And I'll never stop wondering how some folks can hate
other folks so much they'd take it out on a little dog.

I bet if they knew it could come back and haunt them,
though, they'd change.

The Pool Table Caper

Ever since I joined the King Kongs, I wondered why our leader String Bean don't trust Little David.

To me, Little David is the straightest cat on the block. He talks our talk, never puts us down, never comes on like a social worker or a preacher. He makes all us Kongs forget he's thirty years old. And he's an old head Kong himself. He knows what's going down in the streets because he's been there.

His real name is David Lytle, but everybody calls him Little David. Maybe because he's only five feet seven.

Size don't matter. Little David is much man. This is the story of how he proved it to us. Also to Miss Earle, the Director of the Rec Center. After what went down there last month, he's our main man.

But back in June, String Bean didn't want no parts of Little David. Neither did Sunshine, our warlord, or Chop Chop, or Moose, or any of our other members.

I was the only one argued in Little David's favor. I didn't argue too hard, cause I just got in the gang and didn't want to get put out. But I didn't see why we shouldn't drop by the Rec Center like Little David kept asking us.

"He says they got a boss basketball court, a swimming pool, records, TV, all that stuff. Why don't we go check it out?" I asked String.

"Forget it, Dukey," he answered. "It ain't our scene."

"But why not?" I asked. "We ain't got nothing else to do. School is out for the summer, and the Kools ain't giving us no trouble." The Kools are our enemies. They always trying to take over our turf. But they hadn't messed with us in two months.

"We ain't worried about the Kools," said Sunshine, smiling and cracking his knuckles. Sunshine is always smiling. That's how he got his nickname. He smiles broadest when he's about to waste somebody. "We worried about something else," he said.

I didn't ask what. I didn't want to push it too hard. At fourteen, I'm the youngest Kong and the newest. Took me two years building my rep to get in the gang. I had to waste four cats twice my size before String and Sunshine would even look at me. And now I was in, I still had to watch my step or get kicked out. I didn't want that to happen. The gang meant too much to me.

"You like Little David, don't you, Dukey?" String asked softly.

I shrugged. I didn't want to come on too strong. "The cat's all right with me."

"You a fool," said Sunshine.

"No, he just don't ask enough questions," said String. "Like, what happened after that famous rumble between the Kools and the Kongs back in '60? Bloody Easter?"

"Yeah," said Chop Chop. "Five cats died in that rumble. Little David was the Kong warlord. But he didn't get no time for it. He just disappeared."

"And ten, twelve years later, he comes back to the block. Where's he been all that time?" asked String.

"Why don't you ask him?" I said.

String ignored me. "Now he's back," he said, "and he's got that jive job over at the Rec Center. Part time rec leader, part time janitor. Making fifty, maybe sixty a week. But he drives a late model Buick. He wears custom clothes. He's in Tubby's Lounge every night, buying drinks for everybody. Where's he get the coins?"

"And when he's not in Tubby's," said Sunshine, his teeth flashing, "he's hanging out on the corner with us. Why?"

"Maybe he's just friendly," I said, feeling stupid.

"Maybe he's a *cop*," said String. "Or a paid informer."

"Same thing," said Moose.

"Maybe he wants to get us over the Rec Center so he can spy on us. Find out if we got weapons and where we keep 'em. Listen in on our war councils. Learn when we plan to move on the Kools and where."

It made me feel bad, hearing them talk that way about a cat I liked and looked up to. But I didn't get a chance to speak up for him.

"Speak of the devil," said Chop.

"Hang loose," ordered String.

Coming toward us, in a bright red Ban-Lon shirt and matching suede loafers, was Little David.

String gave Little David some skin, and the rest of us did likewise. We slapped palms all around.

"How you doin', sport?" Sunshine asked him, like he hadn't been calling him a stool pigeon thirty seconds ago.

"Oh, you know," Little David answered. "Struggling, as usual. But making it." When he smiles, his eyes crinkle up and look so warm and kind I can't believe he's a stoolie.

"Meeting the Man is a drag," said Moose, expressing how we all feel about working.

"My boss drags me, all right," Little David said, "but she's a lady."

"A fox?" asked Chop.

"A *natural* fox," said Little David, his hands curving a figure 8 in the air. "But she don't know it. Hides it under long droopy skirts, high-necked blouses, big thick eyeglasses. And gets her kicks out of putting me down."

"What you got to do," says Chop, very serious, "is talk some trash to her." Chop is our Number One ladies' man. "Tell her her eyes shine like stars, and her hair has moonbeams in it. Say her walk upsets you, and her figure drives you out to lunch."

"When you've never finished high school," asked Little David, "how do you talk trash to a chick with a master's degree?"

"Ain't no way," said Moose with a groan.

"Now hold it, hold it," says Chop. "Don't give up so easy. Ain't no woman in the world you can't talk to if you use the right approach."

He's about to give Little David a master lesson in talking trash, when String cuts in smoothly. "Say, sport, what you mean, you never finished high school? All those years you were away, we thought you were in college."

"No such luck, man," Little David said. "After that Bloody Easter rumble with the Kools, the judge gave me my choice, jail or the service. I picked the service.

"I was in the Army twelve years. I planned to stay in forever. I figured I didn't have nothing to come back for."

One of String's questions was answered. But he wasn't satisfied. "Why did you?"

"You mean you never noticed my limp?"

We all shook our heads.

Little David pulled up the left leg of his glen plaid bells. The leg was scarred from knee to ankle, and all along the edge of the scar were ugly stitch marks, like dog teeth.

"I stepped on a mine in Nam," he said. "Blew the bone to bits. I got more steel in that leg than bone now, thanks to the U.S. Army." He replaced the pants leg.

"You got a pension too?" String wanted to know.

"First of every month," Little David said, and pulled a Government check from his pocket. He showed it to String, who whistled.

So now String knew where Little David got his extra spending change. I was glad to see so many holes knocked in his theory. But I didn't know if he had given it up.

Chop was still wrestling with Little David's woman problem. "What's your boss lady's name?" he asked.

"Miss Earle."

Chop sounded real disgusted. "Aw, no, man, that ain't no good. I mean her *first* name."

"She won't tell anybody. Just uses the initials L. H. So I sneaked in the office one day and looked it up. It's Lucrezia Hortense. Deal with *that*."

"Ain't no way," Moose said again, and this time *Chop* groaned.

"Anyway, I want to forget about women tonight," Little David said. "I'm in the mood for a strictly stag evening. What I was looking for was a little game of pool. You guys interested?"

String tapped the pocket that held the check. "Gonna give me a chance to win some of that?"

"Name your game," said Little David.

"Bank," said String and grinned as broadly as Sunshine.

I knew why. Bank is a tall man's game, and String Bean has at least a foot on Little David, though he's so skinny they weigh about the same. A short man can stand on tiptoe, he can stretch, he can cuss, and he can pray. Use mojo too if he wants. But nothing will give him the advantage over a tall man in a game of bank pool.

Little David didn't seem worried, though. He led the way, walking with that jaunty little bounce I knew now was a limp.

"Where you going?" String asked as we passed Walker's Billiard Parlor, leaving the noise and the laughter behind us.

"Oh, there's a table over at the Rec Center we can have all to ourselves. And it's free," Little David said.

He had tricked us. The King Kongs were going to the Rec Center after all.

String looked angry, but he didn't say anything. Neither did Sunshine. A deal is a deal.

The Rec Center was new, long and low, with lots of glass and a swimming pool in the yard.

Inside was even better. There was an art show in the hall, and downstairs a dance was going on. I could hear a Temptations record. I know Chop wanted to check out that dance, cause his shoulders were twitching in time to the music. Moose, who is built like one, stared at a poster about wrestling matches. A sign about swimming lessons caught my eye. A lot of other good stuff was on that bulletin board.

But we didn't stop to read. We knew it would be against gang rules. We kept moving in a tight formation behind our leader. We passed a closed door with a sign: MISS L. H. EARLE, DIRECTOR.

Little David led us past that one fast. He unlocked another door, and there we were in this boss poolroom. A full-sized table, cues, balls, racks, lamp with a green shade, everything.

But String didn't say nothing, so we kept quiet too. We lined up against the wall while he ran the balls.

Little David didn't know what he was in for. String is the best pool player on the block. Fast, loose, mean, and always on target. He plans to make a living at it.

We watched String go through his practice run. Bend, sight, shoot, sink the ball, using English to line up his next shot. He only missed two shots.

Little David just waited calmly, leaning on his cue stick, till String finished.

"Want to run a few?" String asked.

Little David shook his head. "Rack 'em."

"We're playing eight-ball, right?" said String. "This five says I win."

"You got you a game," said Little David.

"This," said Sunshine, "is going to be murder." And he grinned like he was enjoying the prospect.

But it wasn't all that easy. Except for height, they were evenly matched. Little David took his time—sighting carefully, sliding his cue back and forth between his fingers. He didn't shoot till he was sure. And he seldom missed. One time he sank four in a row.

String came back with a flashy combination shoot. Nine ball in the side pocket, twelve ball in the far corner.

"You supposed to *announce* a combination, man," Little David told him.

We all knew that was true. Otherwise how would anyone know it wasn't just dumb luck?

But String said, "That's West Coast rules," and went on to sink his next-to-last ball.

We held our breaths. That little black eight ball was

four feet away from the cue ball. From where String stood, it must have looked no bigger than a raisin. He walked around the table three times. He bent and sighted twice.

"Now or never," said Sunshine.

Suddenly String bent over. He bounced that cue ball off the cushion and slam into the eight ball. The eight ball shot down to the end of the table and sank into a corner pocket. The cue ball rolled right behind it, but stopped an inch short of the pocket. If it had sunk, it would have scratched String's shot.

All us King Kongs cheered. Loud enough to raise the roof, cause we'd been holding back our noise all through the tense game.

Little David shook String's hand and left a five-dollar bill in it.

But String gave the money back. "Let it ride on the next game," he said. "You were right. I should have called that combination."

They played again, and *that* time String won fair. We were all a lot more relaxed by then, so we sounded off a lot. Half the fun of pool is sounding on the players, anyway.

Sunshine told String to go get his grandmama to help him make a tough shot. I told Little David to go get a box and stand on it. Then Moose told him he was too old to play against young bloods, and offered to buy him some liniment. Little David said save it for String, *he* was the one who had to bend over. And Chop said, "Hurry up and finish this mess so the *pros* can play."

They took it and ended up smiling at each other like they really meant it. Then they let us have the table.

After String and Little David, Chop was the best. Then me, then Sunshine, and Moose last, cause he's so heavy and clumsy. None of us tried to play bank. We knew it was out of our class. We played nine-ball, fifty cents riding on each pay ball. I won two dollars from Moose and was losing them back to Chop when we heard a knock.

"Open this door," said a woman's crisp voice.

"Stash your cash," Little David said quietly. "And hide your smokes."

Then he unlocked the door.

Miss Lucrezia Hortense Earle stood there.

Miss Earle was about five feet four, light-brownskin, and maybe pretty. Maybe not. Her glasses hid her face, same way her clothes hid her shape. Put her in some foxy togs, she might be saying something. But in that long loose dress, she just looked like somebody's grandma.

And sounded like a grandma, too. "Mr. Lytle, you know it's against the rules to lock this door."

"Sorry, Miss Earle, I forgot," Little David said. "Just locked it out of habit, I guess."

"Do I smell smoke?" she asked, wrinkling up her nose.

Little David pretended to sniff too. "I don't smell anything, Miss Earle."

Miss Earle sniffed some more, but she couldn't prove anything. We had fanned the air too hard with our hands.

Finding no evidence seemed to make her mad.

"Mr. Lytle, please inform these young men that smoking is not permitted here. Neither is coarse talk. I could hear you all the way down the hall. Such language!" She glanced at her watch. "The center closes at nine. You have fifteen minutes."

And she wheeled and marched out like a doll-sized general.

Behind her back, Little David saluted. Sunshine laughed without making a sound.

"Man," said Chop after she was gone, "you got my sympathy. That ain't no woman, it's a machine."

"Pay her no mind," Little David said. "We got all night. *I'm* the one who closes up around here." He locked the door from the inside again.

Pretty soon we were right back in the spirit of the game.

String and Sunshine and the other Kongs didn't say nothing against Little David after that. If they still had their suspicions, they kept them to themselves.

And every night we were over at the Rec Center shooting pool.

String was determined to improve his game and be the best in the city. He took on anybody who would play him. He knocked off most players easy.

The big event every night was his game with Little David after everybody else had gone home. They played for money but were so equal the same money kept changing hands. After two weeks they had each won thirty games.

The rest of us played too. The Kongs were getting a rep as pool champs.

But Sunshine had something else besides pool on his mind.

"While we're in here shooting pool," he told String, "the Kools are tearing our rep to pieces."

It seems the Kools had been bad-mouthing on us ever since we started going to the Rec Center. Telling everybody the Kongs had gone soft and become a jive social gang.

And that wasn't all. They had moved in on our turf, even taken over our corner. They had been seen talking trash to some of our chicks. And they were putting out the word we were scared to fight them.

"String, they selling woof tickets all up and down the block. Saying the Kongs are hiding in the Rec Center, scared to come out and fight."

"Let 'em woof," said String, sighting along his cue. "We'll shut them up later."

"I want to do it *now*," Sunshine urged. "We know the Kools ain't nothing but mouth. But who else knows it? Once we go up side their heads, our rep will be safe. Then we can spend the rest of the summer shooting pool."

"I'm shooting pool *now*," String told him, "and you just messed up my shot. Later for this, Shine. This ain't the time or the place to talk about it."

Meaning, Little David was in the room. The smile left Sunshine's face.

But they must have begun to trust Little David *some*. Else they wouldn't have talked about the Kools at all.

Not with him standing right there waiting his turn.

He spoke up. "You know, ever since Bloody Easter, I don't dig rumbles. And Vietnam *really* cured me of fighting. I figure there must be a better way to settle things." He lined up his shot.

"What you got in mind, Dad?" String asked.

"The Kools think they can play some pool too?"

"Sure," said Sunshine, grinning again. "Just like they think they can fight. But they can't do either. They a jive bunch of big mouths."

"Well," said Little David, "why don't you have a pool contest instead of a rumble?"

He missed his shot, an easy one. I could of sworn he did it on purpose.

"The last two weeks, all of you have improved your games. By now String can beat anybody in the city. But the Kools haven't had the same chance to practice. I bet even Dukey, here, could beat their leader. What's his name?"

"Iceberg," Sunshine said.

"Yeah, Iceberg," Little David repeated. "A jive name for the leader of a jive gang. Call themselves Kools just cause they smoke Kool cigarettes. But they ain't really so cool. I bet String could beat all of them in one day. And not even get tired."

String Bean was smiling. I could see he liked the idea. After he sank three balls in a row and won, he liked it even better.

"Let's set it up," he said. "Shine, you get together with

their warlord. Work out the rules and set a date."

"Next Saturday would be a good time," said Little David. "Before they get in too much practice."

"Solid," said String. "Work on it, Sunshine."

Sunshine said he would, though he looked like he wanted to crack some heads instead.

It was all set up. The King Kongs and the Kool World would fight their battle over a pool table next Saturday. And the turf would belong to the winners.

The word was out that the Kools were working out at Walker's Billiard Parlor. Our practice at the Rec Center got more and more serious. String would take most of the weight for us, so he spent the most time at the table. He practiced high English, low English, bank shots, everything. Soon he was so good he was beating Little David practically every night.

It would have all gone off as planned, if those white rec leaders had left us alone. But they kept coming around and bothering us, trying to get us interested in other things besides pool. Talking about swimming, wrestling, basketball, and tennis, when we had a heavy pool contest coming up.

Frank Fulton was the one who bothered us the most. Fulton had blond hair and wore it so long he looked like a cocker spaniel. He wore blue jeans and T-shirts too and tried to act like one of us.

But he had been to college, like all the other white rec leaders, so he outranked Little David.

And he was rich, so naturally he had a pool table at home and thought he was an expert.

Thursday night, two nights before the contest, Frank Fulton walked in. Just in time to see String beat Little David by banking the eight ball in a corner pocket.

"Bravo!" Fulton cried, real corny. "May I play the winner?"

String didn't answer, but that didn't stop Fulton. "Been hearing a lot about you, sport," he said.

"That so?"

"Yeah, people are saying you're the toughest pool player they've ever seen. I want to find out for myself how good you are."

String shrugged. "Cost you five dollars," he said.

"You play for *money?*" Fulton said, a shocked look on his face.

"What you think? He don't play for kicks," said Sunshine.

"Five dollars a game of bank pool," said String, lighting a cigarette. "Or I'll make it easier for you. Make it a game of nine-ball, dollar a ball on the one, three and six, nine ball pays double."

"Nine-ball it is," said Fulton. "You get first shot. But don't let Miss Earle catch you smoking around here."

String shrugged, stamped out the smoke, and got off three wicked shots in a row. Blip, blip, blip. Three balls sunk, just like that.

Fulton was so shook he flubbed his first shot. After that, he missed so many it was pitiful.

The rest of us Kongs didn't help him much. We sounded off, like we always do when we watch a game. But I think we were rougher than usual because it was a white man playing our leader. We hollered things like "Get your mama to help you!" and "Lend that man a pair of glasses!" and "Better stick to Ping-Pong!"

Fulton turned so red you could see it right through the roots of his hair. And the louder we got, the more shots he missed.

Finally, when he was lining up a real tough one, Chop yelled, "Shut your eyes and pray. Ain't no other way!"

That did it. Frank Fulton threw his cue down on the table.

"Finish the game, man," said String.

"*You* finish it," Fulton said. "I quit. I can't keep my mind on the game. Your buddies make too much noise."

He couldn't stand the heat. Guess he was used to the quiet of his daddy's rec room, with no sound but the hi-fi playing softly. Cat like that wouldn't last five minutes in Walker's Billiard Parlor.

"You owe me some money, man," String said.

"Well, you won't get it. It wasn't a fair game. Besides, I never agreed to gamble."

Sunshine whistled softly. We stepped forward and closed up the gaps between us. When Fulton tried to leave, he faced a solid wall of Kongs.

Little David tried to cool it. "Easy, Fulton," he said. "Don't get excited. These boys are all right. They're friends of mine."

"Let him through," String ordered.

So we stepped aside.

But Fulton hung back. "How do I know they won't hang around outside and wait for me?"

"Because I say so," Little David promised.

Fulton didn't take his word for it, though. In less than two minutes he was back, and Miss Earle was with him.

"Everyone leave this room," she ordered. "From now on, the poolroom is off limits to everyone but staff."

"You don't know what you're doing!" Little David cried. "These are the King Kongs. They have a feud with another gang, the Kool World. They were going to settle it *peacefully*, over this pool table."

"That is not my concern," Miss Earle said.

"I think it is," said Little David. "If you don't let them have a pool contest here, they'll fight somewhere else. Some of them may even get killed."

"Mr. Fulton reported that the boys were gambling and smoking, Mr. Lytle."

"There are worse things than gambling and smoking, Miss Earle."

"Perhaps," she said. "But I can't allow them in my center."

Little David told her where it was at. "When did it become *your* center? It belongs to everybody in the city. What you mean is, you can't allow gang kids to use it. One gang is bad enough. But the thought of *two* gangs here at once scares you to death."

"From what Mr. Fulton said," Miss Earle answered,

"you knew about the gambling, Mr. Lytle. Maybe even took part in it. I could fire you for that."

Little David really blew his cool. "Oh, you could fire me any time. I don't have a degree. I got my education in the streets. That's why I'm the only one around here can talk to these kids."

"The trash has not been emptied tonight, Mr. Lytle," she said and walked away. What a put-down. Reminding him that he was only the janitor.

She walked down the hall and shut herself in her office. Little David went off in another direction, to empty the trash, I guess. Fulton was left to run balls all by himself behind the locked door.

String gave us the "let's split" sign.

We held our war council on the steps of the center.
Everybody had a different idea.

Moose wanted to hide in the bushes and wait for Frank Fulton. Jump him, mess him up, and take String's money.

"No," said String. "He ain't worth the trouble."

I wanted to get some bricks and spray paint, break all the windows in the center and write on all the walls.

String turned that idea down too. He said it was kid stuff.

Chop wanted to kidnap Miss Earle.

"And then what?" String asked. Chop had no answer, so he shut up.

But Sunshine still had the same idea he'd had all along. He didn't care about pool or the Rec Center. He just wanted to waste the Kools. This time, when he talked, String listened.

"They askin' for it, man. They been bad-mouthin' us too long. We got a nationwide rep. We can't let a two-bit gang like them mess it up. I say, let's move on 'em."

"When?" String asked.

"Saturday. Same time you was gonna have that jive pool contest. Only *now* we won't be playing."

"Where?"

"Southwest Playground, cause it divides the turfs."

"What you want to use? Heats, blades, or fists?"

Even in the dark I could see Sunshine's grin. "Everything."

String was for it. I could tell. He was about to say yes, when the door of the Rec Center opened. We fell back in the shadows.

But it was only Little David, leaving after locking up the center. He walked right by us, whistling, like he didn't see us. Something went "clang" when he hit the bottom step. After he was out of sight, I ran and picked it up.

It was a key. String tried it on the front door of the Rec Center. It worked!

"All right, you guys, this is the plan," he said. "Dukey, run get some tools. A hammer, pliers, a screwdriver. Some rope too. Clothesline will do.

"Sunshine, here's the keys to my brother-in-law's truck. It's parked in front of my house. Go get it and drive it back here.

"Chop, go home and open up the big cellar door in front of your house. Wait for us there.

"Everybody else meet back here in twenty minutes, under the poolroom window."

I was the first to get back, cause my assignment was the easiest. I borrowed the tools from my uncle who lives around the corner from the Rec Center and snatched the clothesline out of some lady's back yard.

String was waiting inside the window. "Dukey?" he whispered.

"Yes."

"Toss the tools in here."

By the time I climbed up and crawled in the window he and Moose already had the pool table split in two pieces. In a few more minutes, the two became four.

"I knew this thing came apart," String said. "I *ought* to know. I been studying it long enough. Dukey, Little David has a dolly around here somewhere, for the trash cans. See if you can find it."

I found it, all right. Right next to the furnace.

Sunshine drove the truck up to the back door with the lights out. By that time, the first section of the table was on the dolly and ready to roll.

Moose provided most of the muscle, pushing, while the rest of us pulled. We used the rope to haul the first section up on the truck. Then we went back and got the second piece and the third and the fourth. Also some cues and some balls.

We had started at nine-thirty. By eleven we were unloading the truck in front of Chop's house. Piece by piece, we took the table into his cellar, where String and Moose put it back together again.

It was the Kongs' greatest caper! By midnight we were all set up for a game of pool.

But Sunshine wasn't interested. "About the Kools," he said. "What's it gonna be, pool or war?"

"Play me a game while I think about it," String answered.

Sunshine cussed under his breath. He picked up a cue, though.

But before he could even make one shot, there was a loud knock on the cellar door.

We all had the same thought. *Cops!*

But it was only Little David.

We were so relieved to see it was him, we laughed out loud.

"I was in the mood for some pool," he said, "and something told me, 'Go by Chop's house if you want to find you a game.' "

A shadow crossed String's face. "How'd you find out so quick?"

"I thought I'd left some windows open at the center. I came back to check and saw you leaving."

He patted the table. "Nice job. Took you less than three hours. Still going to have the pool contest with the Kools?"

String was uptight. "What you want to know for?"

But Sunshine was smiling broadly. He took out his knife, opened it, and ran his fingers along the blade to test the edge.

Little David dug this action, all right. "Tell you what." He looked at his watch. "It's midnight Thursday. Give me twenty-four hours to square things with Miss Earle."

"No deal," said Sunshine.

Little David ignored him, cause he knew it was up to String. "These are the terms," he said. "If the table is back where it belongs tomorrow night, no questions will be asked. And the pool contest goes off Saturday on schedule."

"And if she ain't willing?" String asked.

Little David looked grim. "You rumble. Because I failed."

Sunshine said, "String, don't waste time with this cat. How we know he ain't gonna report us to the cops?"

"You must be stone out of your mind, man," Little David told him. "How could I report you? I dropped that key. I'm just as guilty as you are."

"You dropped it *on purpose?* Why?" I cried.

"I knew you guys were in a mood to tear up something. I'd rather see you mess up the center than mess up each other."

That was the moment when String decided to trust Little David all the way. I saw it happen. His face relaxed, and he smiled.

"All right, it's a deal, man," he said. "You got twenty-four hours. I wish you luck, cause you'll need it." He held out the key.

"Keep it," Little David said. "You got to let yourselves in one more time. Remember?"

"Man, you're mighty sure of yourself," said Chop. "You must be forgot that woman ain't human."

"I was on her turf tonight. Tomorrow night I'm going to get her on *mine*. Hang around in front of Tubby's from five-thirty on and dig the happenings."

"How will we get the message?" String asked.

Little David held up two fingers. "If I win, I'll give you the 'Peace' signal.

"And if I lose, I'll signal 'Power.' " He raised a fist.

"Right on," said Sunshine.

Chop was at Tubby's an hour before the rest of us. He didn't want to miss any of the action.

By the time we got there, he really had some news to report.

Little David had come cooling it up the street with Miss Earle hanging on his arm like a dishtowel. Both of them had been togged like models on magazine covers. And he had been calling her "Miss Girl" and getting away with it!

"I think she was mad at him before cause he never asked her out," Chop said. "Now she's happy."

Our mouths were wide open, with no sounds coming out. Chop may be an expert on women, but this was too much.

"Look inside if you don't believe me," he said.

Tubby's has a big picture window that looks out on the street. We crowded around.

There they were in a booth, with their heads close together. Little David was sharp in striped bells and a boss white blazer.

But Miss Earle was the real eyeful. She had on a short yellow dress and big yellow earrings. No sleeves. No stockings. And no eyeglasses. She looked good enough to be in the movies. And she was drinking a champagne cocktail.

"That's her third," Chop whispered.

Our eyes bugged out when Little David put his arm around Miss Earle. Man, did that cat have nerve! She was his *boss*.

But she didn't seem to mind. She didn't see us, either. She was too busy digging every word Little David said.

Little David saw us, though. He winked.

Then, behind her back, he held up two fingers in a V. The peace signal!

We answered it with five raised fists. Because now we only had one problem. Making the Kools understand that the Rec Center was our turf, not theirs.

Course, any time they wanted to be our *guests*, like tomorrow, we'd treat them fine.

Debut

"Hold *still*, Judy," Mrs. Simmons said around the spray of pins that protruded dangerously from her mouth. She gave the thirtieth tug to the tight sash at the waist of the dress. "Now walk over there and turn around slowly."

The dress, Judy's first long one, was white organdy over taffeta, with spaghetti straps that bared her round brown shoulders and a wide sash that cascaded in a butterfly effect behind. It was a dream, but Judy was sick and tired of the endless fittings she had endured so that she might wear it at the Debutantes' Ball. Her thoughts leaped ahead to the ball itself . . .

"*Slowly*, I said!" Mrs. Simmons' dark, angular face was always grim, but now it was screwed into an expression resembling a prune. Judy, starting nervously, began to revolve by moving her feet an inch at a time.

Her mother watched her critically. "No, it's still not right. I'll just have to rip out that waistline seam again."

"Oh, Mother!" Judy's impatience slipped out at last. "Nobody's going to notice all those little details."

"They will too. They'll be watching you every minute, hoping to see something wrong. You've got to be the *best*. Can't you get that through your head?" Mrs. Simmons gave a sigh of despair. "You better start noticin' 'all those little details' yourself. I can't do it for you all your life. Now turn around and stand up straight."

"Oh, Mother," Judy said, close to tears from being made to turn and pose while her feet itched to be dancing, "I can't stand it anymore!"

"You can't stand it, huh? How do you think *I* feel?" Mrs. Simmons said in her harshest tone.

Judy was immediately ashamed, remembering the weeks her mother had spent at the sewing machine, pricking her already tattered fingers with needles and pins, and the great weight of sacrifice that had been borne on Mrs. Simmons' shoulders for the past two years so that Judy might bare hers at the ball.

"All right, take it off," her mother said. "I'm going to take it up the street to Mrs. Berry and let her help me. It's got to be right or I won't let you leave the house."

"Can't we just leave it the way it is, Mother?" Judy pleaded without hope of success. "I think it's perfect."

"You would," Mrs. Simmons said tartly as she folded the dress and prepared to bear it out of the room. "Sometimes I think I'll never get it through your head. You got to look just right and act just right. That Rose Griffin and those other girls can afford to be careless, maybe, but you can't. You're gonna be the darkest, poorest one there."

Judy shivered in her new lace bra and her old, childish

knit snuggies. "You make it sound like a battle I'm going to instead of just a dance."

"It is a battle," her mother said firmly. "It starts tonight and it goes on for the rest of your life. The battle to hold your head up and get someplace and be somebody. We've done all we can for you, your father and I. Now you've got to start fighting some on your own." She gave Judy a slight smile; her voice softened a little. "You'll do all right, don't worry. Try and get some rest this afternoon. And don't mess up your hair."

"All right, Mother," Judy said listlessly.

She did not really think her father had much to do with anything that happened to her. It was her mother who had ingratiated her way into the Gay Charmers two years ago, taking all sorts of humiliation from the better-dressed, better-off, lighter-skinned women, humbly making and mending their dresses, fixing food for their meetings, addressing more mail and selling more tickets than anyone else. The club had put it off as long as they could, but finally they had to admit Mrs. Simmons to membership because she worked so hard. And that meant, of course, that Judy would be on the list for this year's ball.

Her father, a quiet carpenter who had given up any other ambitions years ago, did not think much of black society or his wife's fierce determination to launch Judy into it. "Just keep clean and be decent," he would say. "That's all anybody has to do."

Her mother always answered, "If that's all *I* did we'd still be on relief," and he would shut up with shame over the years when he had been laid off repeatedly and her day work and sewing had kept them going. Now he had steady work, but she refused to quit—as if she expected it to end at any moment. The intense energy that burned in Mrs. Simmons' large dark eyes had scorched her features into permanent irony. She worked day and night and spent her spare time scheming and planning. Whatever her personal ambitions had been, Judy knew she blamed Mr. Simmons for their failure. Now all her schemes revolved around their only child.

Judy went to her mother's window and watched her stride down the street with the dress until she was hidden by the high brick wall that went around two sides of their house. Then she returned to her own room. She did not get dressed because she was afraid of pulling a sweater over her hair—her mother would notice the difference even if it looked all right to Judy—and because she was afraid that doing anything, even getting dressed, might push her into the battle.

She drew a stool up to her window and looked out. She had no real view, but she liked her room. The wall hid the crowded tenement houses beyond the alley, and from its cracks and bumps and depressions she could construct any imaginary landscape she chose. It was how she had spent most of the free hours of her dreamy adolescence.

"Hey, can I go?"

It was the voice of an invisible boy in the alley. As another boy chuckled, Judy recognized the familiar ritual; if you said yes, they said, "Can I go with you?" It had been tried on her dozens of times. She always walked past, head in the air, as if she had not heard. Her mother said that was the only thing to do; if they knew she was a lady, they wouldn't dare bother her. But this time a girl's voice, cool and assured, answered.

"If you think you big enough," it said.

It was Lucy Mae Watkins. Judy could picture her standing there in a tight dress with bright, brazen eyes.

"I'm big enough to give you a baby," the boy answered.

Judy would die if a boy ever spoke to her like that, but she knew Lucy Mae could handle it. Lucy Mae could handle all the boys, even if they ganged up on her, because she had been born knowing something other girls had to learn.

"Aw, you ain't big enough to give me a shoe shine," she told him.

"Come here and I'll show you how big I am," the boy said.

Lucy Mae laughed. "What I'm puttin' down is too strong for little boys like you."

"Come here a minute, baby," the first boy said. "I got a cigarette for you."

"Aw, I ain't studyin' your cigarettes," Lucy Mae answered. But her voice was closer, directly below Judy. There were the sounds of a scuffle and Lucy Mae's muffled laughter. When she spoke, her voice sounded raw and cross. "Come on now, boy. Cut it out and give me the cigarette." There was more scuffling and the sharp crack of a slap, and then Lucy Mae said, "Cut it out, I said. Just for that I'm gonna take 'em all." The clack of high heels rang down the sidewalk with a boy's clumsy shoes in pursuit.

Judy realized that there were three of them down there. "Let her go, Buster," one said. "You can't catch her now."

"Aw, shoot, man, she took the whole pack," the one called Buster complained.

"That'll learn you!" Lucy Mae's voice mocked from down the street. "Don't mess with nothin' you can't handle."

"Hey, Lucy Mae. Hey, I heard Rudy Grant already gave you a baby," the second boy called out.

"Yeah. Is that true, Lucy Mae?" the youngest one yelled.

There was no answer. She must be a block away by now.

For a moment the hidden boys were silent; then one of them guffawed directly below Judy, and the other two joined in the secret male laughter that was oddly high-pitched and feminine.

"Aw man, I don't know what you all laughin' about," Buster finally grumbled. "That girl took all my cigarettes. You got some, Leroy?"

"Naw," the second boy said.

"Me neither," said the third one.

"What we gonna do? I ain't got but fifteen cent. Shoot, I want more than a feel for a pack of cigarettes." There was an unpleasant whine in Buster's voice. "If she pass by here again, we gonna jump her, you hear?"

"Sure, man," the boy called Leroy said. "The three of us can grab her easy."

"Then we can all three of us have some fun. Oh, *yeah*, man," the youngest boy said. He sounded as if he might be about thirteen.

Leroy said, "We oughta get Roland and J.T. too. For a whole pack of cigarettes she oughta treat all five of us."

"Aw, man, why tell Roland and J.T.?" the youngest voice whined. "They ain't in it. Them was *our* cigarettes."

"They was *my* cigarettes, you mean," Buster said with authority. "You guys better quit it before I decide to cut you out."

"Oh, man, don't do that. We with you, you know that."

"Sure, Buster, we your aces, man."

"All right, that's better." There was a minute of silence.

Then, "What we gonna do with the girl, Buster?" the youngest one wanted to know.

"When she come back we gonna jump her, man. We gonna jump her and grab her. Then we gonna turn her every way but loose." He went on, spinning a fantasy that got wilder each time he retold it, until it became so secret that their voices dropped to a low indistinct murmur punctuated by laughter. Now and then Judy could distinguish the word "girl" or the other word they used for it. These words always produced the loudest guffaws of all.

She shook off her fear with the thought that Lucy Mae was too smart to pass there again today. She had heard them at their dirty talk in the alley before and had always been successful in ignoring it. It had nothing to do with her; the wall protected her from their kind. All the ugliness was on their side of it, and this side was hers to fill with beauty.

She turned on her radio to shut them out completely and began to weave her tapestry to its music. More for practice than anything else, she started by picturing the maps of the places to which she intended to travel, then went on to the faces of her friends. Rose Griffin's sharp, Indian profile appeared on the wall. Her coloring was like an Indian's too, and her hair was straight and glossy. Judy's hair had been "done" four days ago so that tonight it would be "old" enough to have a gloss as natural-looking as Rose's. But Rose, in spite of her handsome looks, was silly. Her voice broke constantly into high-pitched giggles, and she became even sillier and more nervous around boys.

Judy was not sure that she knew how to act around boys either. The sisters kept boys and girls apart at the Catholic school where her parents sent her to keep her away from low-class kids. But she felt that she knew a secret: Tonight, in that dress, she would be transformed into a poised princess. Tonight all the college boys her mother described so eagerly would rush to dance with her. And then from somewhere *the* boy would appear.

She did not know his name. She neither knew nor cared whether he went to college. But she imagined that there would be awe and diffidence in his manner as he bent to kiss her hand . . .

A waltz swelled from the radio. The wall, turning blue in deepening twilight, came alive with whirling figures. Judy rose and began to go through the steps she had re-hearsed for so many weeks. She swirled with a practiced smile on her face, holding an imaginary skirt at her side, turned, dipped, and flicked on her bedside lamp without missing a fraction of the beat. Faster and faster she danced with her imaginary partner, to an inner music that was better than the sounds on the radio. She was "coming out," and tonight the world would discover what it had been waiting for all these years.

"Aw, git it, baby." She ignored it as she would ignore the crowds that lined the streets to watch her pass on her way to the ball.

"Aw, do your number." She waltzed on, safe on her side of the wall.

"Can I come up there and do it with you?"

At this she stopped, paralyzed. Somehow they had come over the wall or around it and into her room.

"Man, I sure like the view from here," the youngest boy said. "How come we never tried this view before?"

She came to life, ran quickly to the lamp, and turned it off; but not before Buster said, "Yeah, and the back view is fine, too."

"Aw, she turned off the light," a voice complained.

"Put it on again, baby, we don't mean no harm."

"Let us see you dance some more. I bet you can really do it."

"Yeah, I bet she can shimmy on down."

"You know it, man."

"Come on down here, baby," Buster's voice urged softly, dangerously. "I got a cigarette for you."

"Yeah, and he got something else for you, too."

Judy, flattened against her closet door, gradually lost her urge to scream. She realized that she was shivering in her underwear. Taking a deep breath, she opened the closet door and found her robe. She thought of going to the window and yelling down, "You don't have a thing I want. Do you understand?" But she had more important things to do.

Wrapping her hair in a protective chamois cloth, she ran a full steaming tub and dumped in half a bottle of her mother's favorite cologne. At first she scrubbed herself furiously, irritating her skin. But finally she stopped, knowing she would never be able to get cleaner than this again. She could not wash away the thing they considered dirty, the thing that made them pronounce "girl" in the same way as the other four-letter words they wrote on the wall in the alley. It was part of her, just as it was part of her mother and Rose Griffin and Lucy Mae. She relaxed then because it was true that the boys in the alley did not have a thing she wanted. She had what they wanted, and the knowledge replaced her shame with a strange, calm feeling of power.

After her bath she splashed on more cologne and spent forty minutes on her makeup, erasing and retracing her eyebrows six times until she was satisfied. She went to her mother's room then and found the dress, finished and freshly pressed, on its hanger.

When Mrs. Simmons came upstairs to help her daughter, she found her sitting on the bench before the vanity mirror as if it were a throne. She looked young and arrogant and beautiful and perfect and cold.

"Why, you're dressed already," Mrs. Simmons said in surprise. While she stared, Judy rose with perfect, icy grace and glided to the center of the room. She stood there motionless as a mannequin.

"I want you to fix the hem, Mother," she directed. "It's still uneven in back."

Her mother went down obediently on her knees, muttering, "It looks all right to me." She put in a couple of pins. "That better?"

"Yes," Judy said with a brief glance at the mirror. "You'll have to sew it on me, Mother. I can't take it off now. I'd ruin my hair."

Mrs. Simmons went to fetch her sewing things, returned, and surveyed her daughter. "You sure did a good job on yourself, I must say," she admitted grudgingly. "Can't find a thing to complain about. You'll look as good as anybody there."

"Of course, Mother," Judy said as her mother knelt and sewed. "I don't know what you were so worried about." Her secret feeling of confidence had returned, stronger than ever, but the evening ahead was no longer the vague fantasy she had pictured on the wall. It had hard, clear outlines leading up to a definite goal. She would be the belle of the ball because she knew more than Rose Griffin and her silly friends, more than her mother, more, even, than Lucy Mae, because she knew better than to settle for a mere pack of cigarettes.

"There," her mother said, breaking the thread. She got up. "I never expected to get you ready this early. Ernest Lee won't be here for another hour."

"That silly Ernest Lee," Judy said, with a new contempt in her young voice. Until tonight she had been pleased by the thought of going to the dance with Ernest Lee. He was nice, she felt comfortable with him, and he might even be the awestruck boy of her dream. He was a dark, serious neighborhood boy who could not afford to go to college. Mrs. Simmons had reluctantly selected him to take Judy to the dance because all the Gay Charmers' sons were spoken for.

Now, with an undertone of excitement, Judy said, "I'm going to ditch him after the first dance, Mother. You'll see. I'm going to come home with one of the college boys."

"It's very nice, Ernest Lee," she told him an hour later when he handed her the white orchid, "but it's rather small. I'm going to wear it on my wrist, if you don't mind." And then, dazzling him with a smile of sweetest cruelty, she stepped back and waited while he fumbled with the door.

Two's Enough of a Crowd

I used to blame all my troubles on being a nondancer. I thought if I could learn to wiggle and shake, I'd be popular.

One flashy minute on the floor, and whammo! I'd be the Dream Lover. Instead of a tall, skinny, nervous cat who's always trying to disappear into a wall.

It took Amy to show me I was different in other ways too.

Like my name. Most black cats are named James or William or Leroy. And they're called Cool Breeze or Poor Boy or Pots and Pans.

Nobody black is named Maurice. Except me. And nobody ever called me anything else.

(Of course, nobody black is named *Amy*, either. Now that there's two of us, it's not so bad.)

But in the old days, I felt mighty sorry for myself. I thought I was the only black person in the world with two left feet and no sense of rhythm.

If you're white, you don't have to dance. All you got

to do is talk that talk, program them computers, and count that money.

But to be black and a nondancer is like being a blind brain surgeon. Or a one-armed violinist.

Most black kids are born knowing how to dance. They boogaloo into this world and funky chicken into their mothers' arms. Even in my family.

At twelve months my little brother started walking. At fourteen months, he was slopping. I was so disgusted, I never spoke to the little monster again.

Here I thought my bad dancing was something I'd *inherited*, like a long head and pointed ears.

Don't tell me dancing isn't important. Old folks always say that. They say not dancing leaves you more time to study. Well, that just shows how much *they* know. I'd sell my straight A average tomorrow if I could do the monkey.

Don't tell me to take dancing lessons, either. I tried. I found out three things.

One, only the first lesson is free. After that, they charge you a fortune.

Two, they only teach nowhere dances like the fox-trot and the samba.

Three, ain't no school in the world can teach soul dancing. Sure, they can draw marks on the floor to show where your feet go. But those marks don't show you how to move the rest of your body. And *that's* where it's at, baby.

The knees and the hips and the waist and the arms are

all part of the action. And they all got to move *together*. You're either born knowing how, or you're not. If you got it, flaunt it.

If you haven't got it, hide behind the biggest piece of furniture. Which is what I usually do at parties.

At Keeno Robinson's Christmas party, I headed for the Christmas tree as soon as the first record started playing. The tree was only five feet high, and I'm six-one. But by scrunching down, I managed to hide.

Then I peered through the branches. The floor was frantic. Every couple deserved to be on TV. But the best were Stretch Hankins and LaTanya Harris.

LaTanya is the world's foxiest chick. She wears extra hair, false eyelashes and skin-tight sweaters. I don't really like her. But I'd have given anything to dance with her the way Stretch was doing.

The only time I danced with LaTanya, I stepped on her foot. She laughed at me. I haven't asked her to dance since.

I thought I was the only one at the party not dancing. Then I spotted someone else. I couldn't believe my eyes.

Over in the opposite corner sat this *beautiful* girl. All by herself. *Reading.*

Crossing the floor to get to her wasn't easy. It was like walking through a roomful of guided missiles. But I managed to get there without any bruises.

She looked just as good close up. And it was all real. Hair, eyelashes, everything. "What's your name?" I asked.

"Amy. Amy Livingston."

I told her mine. Then I asked what she was reading.

"Oh, just a book."

"Why did you hide it when I came over?"

"I thought you might laugh at me. It's not relevant."

Now, "relevant" is a very big word in our crowd. If a thing isn't relevant, it's nowhere. As far as I can figure out, "relevant" means something you know already. Like how to comb a natural, and where to buy neck bones.

I finally got the title out of her. *Green Mansions*, by W. H. Hudson.

"It's just a romantic story about a girl who lives in the woods. There aren't any black people in it or anything. It isn't even about anything that could have really happened. It's not at *all* relevant."

"Do you like it?" I asked.

"Very much."

"Well then," I said, "it's relevant to *you*."

She smiled. It was delightful. All pearls and dimples. "Thank you for saying that. I never thought of that before."

"But why aren't you dancing?" I wanted to know.

"Oh, nobody ever asks me to dance." She wasn't feeling sorry for herself. She just said it straight. Like, "Oh, it never rains around here in October."

But she had to be putting me on. She looked like somebody on a magazine cover.

Idiot that I am, I couldn't resist. "Well, someone is now." Here we go, Mister Clumsy Chump, I thought.

"We'll have to wait for a slow record," she said. And looked down sideways, toward her right foot.

I saw that she had on a heavy, built-up shoe.

"I was born with one leg shorter than the other," she explained.

"Just be glad you were born," I said. It came out sounding hard and tough. I hadn't meant it to.

So I added, "Because *I* am."

I got the full, dazzling smile that time. It almost blinded me.

"Oh, what a nice thing to say. I *am* glad. Especially now that I can walk. I couldn't always, you know."

The athletes and acrobats were finally taking a rest. A slow record started playing. And we started moving around the floor.

It was just as easy as that. I found I didn't have to worry about the beat. She dragged one foot slowly. So I dragged both of mine. It left me free to concentrate on other things, like her perfume. It smelled like lilacs, and got me a little drunk.

"You're a great dancer," she said afterward.

Now, anyone who tells me *that* has a friend for life. But the trouble with me is I'm honest.

"Girl, you're a lovely liar," I said. "I can't dance at all."

"Really?" she said with a mischievous grin. "What else can't you do?"

I gave it some serious thought. Finally I admitted, "I can't curse."

It's quite a problem. Most of my friends turn the air blue with every other sentence. But *my* folks are so strict, I have trouble saying heck and darn.

"You think that's bad? I can't even use *slang*," she said.

She really had my sympathy. First of all, it's not "slang," it's "jive talk." And in our crowd, it's your first language. English is your second.

"I had eight operations," she explained. "I spent four years in the hospital, off and on. Nobody to talk to but white doctors and nurses. Now all the kids say I talk white. They make fun of me. So I mostly keep quiet."

"I love the way you talk. Don't you dare stop," I said.

It was jungle time again. James Brown was grunting and shouting over three speakers. And LaTanya was going into her act. She danced so violently you'd have thought she was in a hurricane.

Keeno appointed himself a one-man cheering section. "Work out, mama," he urged. "Take it easy, but go greasy. Shake it but don't break it, cause if you bruise it, you can't use it! Oh, I feel so *attitudinous!* My vines are fine, my choppers shine, I'm full of wine, and this pad is *mine!* Pull back your jibs, peasants, and let me pass! OobydoobyshoobyOW!"

"I think he's happy," I translated for Amy.

"Monkeys love bananas. Maybe somebody just gave him one," she said with a giggle.

I laughed too. Suddenly, the crowd at the party didn't seem like the World's Most Important People. They were just people.

Another person was what made the difference. Or so I was discovering. When you're alone, the center of the crowd seems like the only place to be.

But when there are two of you, you can sit back and watch without feeling left out. You feel very cozy because you've got your *own* crowd.

"Do you like soul food?" I asked. Some platters were appearing.

"I hate it," she said. "All that grease. *Ugh*."

My sentiments exactly. Why had I been forcing myself to swallow it all those years?

Because I had been alone, that's why. And, alone, I didn't have the courage to say "no thank you."

I was getting curious about this girl. I asked her more questions. "Do you hate honkies?"

"What are they?" she asked.

Too much. Too everlasting much. I explained.

She shuddered. "Oh, no. My doctor is white. He *helped* me. Besides, I don't hate anybody."

"But don't you feel oppressed?"

"I guess I *should*," she said, looking troubled. "But the truth is, I feel free as a bird. Ever since I started walking."

"Do you like James Brown?" was my next question.

"No," she admitted. "He doesn't sing. He screams."

Now, James Brown is the High Priest of What's Happening. The Sultan of Soul. Not liking him is like drawing a funny mustache on a picture of Malcolm X.

I cheered her courage. "Hooray. Who *is* your favorite musician?"

"Schubert," she said. "And after him, Brahms."

Too unbelievable much! "What else do you like that's unrelevant?"

"The word is *irrelevant*," she corrected gently. "And the answer is 'everything.' "

The steamy odor of stewed innards was filling Keeno's rec room. Our host was about to pass out the chitlins. "Wrinkled steaks, everybody!" he hollered gleefully.

"It's not polite to refuse food," I said. "Let's go, before they make us *eat* those horrible things."

Boy, I felt brave. And free. Like it was 1865, and I'd just kicked off my chains. The ones put on me by my own people.

Amy's house was just like Amy. Different. There were no zebra-striped pillows. No plaster heads of Africans. No orange ceramic cats. Strangest of all, no plastic slipcovers. And no wall-to-wall Spanish-style stereo.

Just worn, comfortable furniture. Old, soft rugs. Lots of books. And a fine, foreign turntable sitting on top of a speaker.

It worked too, which is more than I can say for some stereos. The *Great Symphony* by Schubert lived up to its name. So did the *Fantastic* one by Berlioz.

When they had finished playing, I said, "You're a brave girl, to be so different."

"Not really," she said. "If you're different, you just *are*. You can't be any other way. You have no choice."

So it was as simple as that! After all those years of hiding and pretending to be like the crowd. This girl was amazing.

"But how did you get to be this way?"

"I told you. I had all those operations. They put me behind in school. I've never had much time to run with the crowd. I have to read and study a lot, if I want to catch up and go to college."

"What do you plan to take up? Black studies?"

"Promise not to tell."

I promised.

"English writers. The early ones. Like Chaucer."

Now, how irrelevant can you get? I almost kissed her *then*. "Why did you make me promise not to tell?" I asked.

"Because they'd put me down."

"Who?"

"Keeno. And Cool Breeze. And Sheryl. And Stretch. And LaTanya."

"Well, who put them in charge of the world?" I asked. "Who made *them* the dictators?"

"Nobody. But they *are*."

"Let me tell you about me," I said. "I have this thing about cells and germs. I love to look at them under a microscope."

"Maybe you'll discover a cure for sickle cell anemia. That's a disease only black people have. That would be relevant."

"Maybe *you'll* discover Chaucer was black."

We laughed ourselves absolutely silly over that one.

Then we got serious. We promised never to let the others know our secrets. Not that we're scared or ashamed. It's just more fun that way.

"Listen, Amy," I said. "This spring my class is having a prom. Not my scene at all. I wasn't planning to go. But I will if you'll go with me."

"I'd love to, Maurice," she said. She made my name sound better than a nickname. When all those years, I'd wished for one.

"I warn you," I said. "I can't do the slop, the wobble, the monkey, or the funky chicken."

"My favorite dance," she said, "is the waltz."

I *had* to kiss her that time. First, for being so different. Second, for showing me I was, too. Third, for proving it didn't matter. Because there were *two* of us now, and we didn't need the dictators. We didn't need to dance, either. How important is dancing, compared to walking?

So we'll go to the prom. And when the others rap and rave, we'll keep quiet. While they jump and shake, we'll sit on the sidelines and smile. And keep our secrets.

Because we've found out that nothing's as relevant as love.

Come Out of That Corner

Out in the center of the floor there was plenty of room, but there they stayed. Huddled down there in that same old corner, dancing in a space so confined there was barely room for four couples, let alone ten. And the grim, serious way they danced in their incongruously bright clothes. Like a solemn procession, moving in and out in formal patterns, now rapidly, now sedately, as the music changed. Never moving out of that corner. *Their* corner.

Damn you, Carlie thought, watching them from above. *Come out of that corner*. She leaned against the rail edging the gallery of the gym. A rock recording blared out over the PA system. In the scooped-out oval fifteen feet below, more than a hundred couples made bright, jerky, moving patterns. She ignored them, concentrating all her fury on the small knot of dancers in the corner.

Once, a month ago, she'd been down there with them. Once only, urged by Rosalinda. Which one would dance with her? Baby-faced, quick-witted Harvey Roper, all of five feet tall, while she was five-eight? Jackie Jamison, with his big feet, big ears, sleepy voice, broad sweet slow-witted smile? Teddy Harper, the farmer's son, tall and awkward in tight denims? Hoping, she'd smiled brightly at all of them as they stood around shuffling their feet, eyeing her from a distance, trying to make conversation.

"Where you been keepin' yourself, Carlie?"

"Same old place, I guess."

How she'd hoped that was the right answer. But their eyes, catching sudden fire with the hot blare of music, were not for her. They were for each other, and she'd stepped back, marveling as they paired off and one became two, two became twenty, twenty became one, a field of weeds in the wind. For God's sake, she'd whispered. You're beautiful! Get out in the middle of the floor!

Rosalinda had stayed with her, though. Loyal little Rosalinda. "Let me see your motion," she'd said, pulling Carlie into the deepest recess of the corner, where no one would notice two girls dancing together. "You're stiff, girl, stiff! Get loose! Shake it a little!" The harder Carlie tried to follow Rosalinda's easy movements, the more she stumbled. Finally Rosalinda just stood there sadly shaking her head. "Lord! You about the *stiffest* sister I ever seen!"

But she'd yelled to the boys, belligerent hands on her hips: "What's the matter with you? Come on over here and dance with Carlie!" Finally Harvey came over sheepishly and offered his hand. Charity.

Carlie remembered how she'd pleaded a headache then

and fled. She wondered briefly why she bothered to come to the Friday lunch hour dances at all. Some perverse anger brought her there every week to watch and wait and seethe inside, though she would never be missed if she stayed away.

A friendly voice interrupted her.

"Excuse me. How about the next dance?" it said, incredibly.

She wheeled to face a smiling boy, an extended hand. A shock of cloudy brown hair, blue eyes, a friendly smile. Who? Who? Of course. The new boy, in school less than a week. In her history class, quiet, polite. "May I borrow your notes, please? Thanks." Paul Rensler.

She returned his smile just in time. "Why, certainly," she said, giving him her hand.

"They didn't dance like this where I came from," he was saying, as they went down the stairs. "You'll have to show me how."

She barely heard him. A strange exultation swept her as she led him to the very center before turning to his arms.

"I said, you'll have to show me," he repeated. "Carlotta. Is that right?"

"Carlie they call me," she murmured.

"You're a great dancer, Carlie," he said, leading her around the floor.

She smiled at him, nodding when he spoke, following him well, but her mind was far away. Over her shoulder she caught sight of the little group in the corner, staring and talking among themselves. I don't care, she thought, lifted to new heights by their disapproval. I don't care what any of you think.

Head high, she soared, her feet barely touching the floor. Careful, now. Don't spoil it yourself. The others will do it for you soon enough. Say something. Anything.

"How do you like it here?" she said softly.

"Fine, I guess. I don't know too many people yet."

That's for sure, she thought. Or you'd never have asked me to dance.

"So I guess I'll start with you. Where do you live, Carlie?"

"Somerton," she said cautiously. "About five miles down."

"Gee, that's too bad. I mean—you're so far away, and I'm right here in Bloker, down on Old Mill Road. Family decided to move here from upstate, and here I am."

"Yes," she said, smiling gently. "Here you are." It was a faster tune now, and she whirled with the beat, following him without effort. The smile on her face began to feel strained, like a pasted-on smile. She kept it there, though. And kept the head up. You're out here now, Carlie. Stay out here as long as you can.

"Do they have these dances every week?"

"Yes, Paul." The panic was beginning. *Run*, it said. She felt it tugging at the vital centers of her body.

"They have big dances too, don't they? When's this junior formal?"

"That's next Saturday night, I think." *Run*, it said, more urgently.

"Would it be too much nerve to ask—well, are you doing anything that night?"

Run, it screamed. *Run somewhere and hide while you have a chance.*

"Paul, that's awfully nice of you," she said, controlling her voice carefully. "Thanks a lot. But I'm tied up."

"Sure, I can understand that, " he said pleasantly. "Well . . . maybe you'll change your mind."

The fast tune was ending, and a slow one was taking its place without a break. *Run.* "You'll have to excuse me, Paul. I'm—headache—dizzy—not feeling well."

"What? Oh, I'm sorry." His kind voice and troubled eyes expressed genuine concern.

"Nothing, really. Guess I'm just tired. But thanks a lot. That was fun." It was a battle to keep the voice gay, to keep from breaking loose and running.

"Thank *you*," he said, releasing her politely. "See you later, Carlie."

She hurried blindly off the floor. You wouldn't thank me if you knew. You're so nice. So nice. And you'll never be nice any more. She ran up the stairs, not quite fast enough to miss a girl's remark as she passed the corner:

"Thinks she's cute. Hangin' out with the wheat people."

Had it been Rosalinda or one of the others? She didn't pause to find out. She rushed out the girls' exit, past the deserted showers. Thank heaven the girls' room was empty. Breathing hard, she put down her small handbag (fine polished calf), took a washcloth and tiny cake of soap out of her vanity case (monogrammed), and washed her face. You couldn't carry it off, she told the girl in the mirror. Well, but I'm not sorry, she answered. I'm glad. I don't like corners. I don't want to be with people who hide in corners. I don't want to dance with Harvey or Teddy or Jackie anyway. All right, I *do*. But they don't want to dance with me.

She moved abruptly from the mirror when Ellen Jacobs and Hilda Hammer came in. They were both in her homeroom. She was used to their cold, incurious glances, but this time she wanted to be the one who refused to speak.

"Hello," Ellen said. She stared at Carlie strangely until Hilda nudged her. They both turned to the mirror. Carlie watched Hilda's reflection grimace as she put on pink lipstick.

"Never knew you were such a good dancer, Carlie," she mouthed around the lipstick. "Been hiding your talents."

Carlie moved a step backward, nearer the wall where they could not see her reflection in the mirror. "Oh, I got talents I ain't *used* yet," she said in a drawl exactly like Rosalinda's. Hilda stifled a giggle, joined by Ellen a moment later. Leaning against the wall, Carlie opened her French book and pretended to be absorbed. Soon they went back to their conversation. Something about the vote for the most popular girl in school, which Hilda was sure to win . . .

Où est ma chère amie? Here you are, Ellen. I used to

play house in your kitchen, summers a long time ago. When lunchtime came you wouldn't let me go home, and your mother would spread sweet butter on Jewish rye bread and give us each a big slice. *Elle est allée au lycée.* You used to play in my back yard, Hilda. You were always the bewitched princess, and your brother Max was the brave knight, and I was the evil witch who put the spell on you. Even then I knew I could never be the princess . . . only the witch. Is that why you're afraid of me now? Or is it that you still remember the time we picked the forsythia bush clean . . . and my mother came out and spanked us both?

Mother. Who had first straightened Carlie out on the facts of life. "Stop running after your little chums, Carlotta. Those friendships may not continue once you're in high school."

"Why?"

"Do I really have to go into that?" her mother had said wearily. "Just don't run after them. Let them come to you. And don't be surprised if they stay away."

Why had they picked this particular suburb, a million miles from nowhere, to build that house, *their* corner, a hundred feet back from the road?

For your sake, dear, Mother always said calmly. *We wanted the best for you.*

The best was this high school, a regional high school, drawing kids from fifteen different towns. Five hundred of the others, two dozen of her kind, who were not, as Mother always pointed out, her kind at all.

Once she'd dragged Rosalinda home from school with her, and immediately regretted it. She'd seemed so small, so scared, so *different* somehow in Carlie's house. "Is it all right to walk on these rugs?" She'd shrunk into herself, and walked on tiptoe, and Carlie had been embarrassed —and ashamed of her embarrassment. Never again would she put Rosalinda or anyone else through such torture. Her father meant well, but his voice rang out as accusingly in the kitchen as in the courtroom. Her mother was kind, but her kindness masqueraded behind the grand manner of the ladies whose kitchens Rosalinda's mother scrubbed.

It was months since she'd sneaked out to one of Rosalinda's parties. The last time, she'd sat quietly in a corner of the dim cellar, listening to the others' hip language, trying to learn, though it was harder for her than French, watching the dark shapes dance tirelessly in the glow of a red bulb. Only when they began to stumble over her as if she were furniture had she moved, groping her way along the wall until she nearly fell over another couple, the girl giggling, the boy cursing.

Now Carlie went nowhere, and no one came to her.

The girls had gone, leaving echoes of shrill laughter in the dank air of the washroom. Carlie looked herself over in the mirror. Eyes slightly red, she saw, but a face otherwise quite presentable, quite pretty. Except, in this strong light, the skin was a trifle more golden than Ellen's or Hilda's, the dark hair a little more thickly and tightly curled. And, if you looked from the proper angle, you caught a certain something about the features—the sharp planes melting into something softer, fuller, less defined. Miss In Between. Lord, who am I? Then she spoke sternly to the girl in the mirror. "You know perfectly well who you are. Even if Paul doesn't."

Behind hers, a more definite face materialized in the mirror. Full lips, flat nose and a super bad natural that added four inches in height. The expression was unusually serious, but the face was unmistakably Rosalinda's.

"Got to school you, girl," she said. "We don't dance with white boys."

"Is there a law?" Carlie tossed off with a flippancy she did not feel.

"No. We just don't, that's all."

Carlie could not erase the rebellious streak that made her question everything. "Why not?"

Rosalinda's devilish grin returned for an instant. "For one thing, they can't half dance. They hop around like jackrabbits, always off the beat."

Carlie knew all that. Her own timing also left something to be desired, though. "You must have a better reason."

"Girl, don't you know *nothin'?*"

Latin, French, a hundred lines of Longfellow—they hardly helped in this situation. Carlie shook her head miserably.

Rosalinda shook hers, too, in despair. "How'm I gonna 'splain it to you, then? Look. Our boys can't dance with their girls."

"Why not?" Carlie asked again.

"Cause they'd get *killed*, fool."

"Oh, Rosalinda, really. This isn't Mississippi. This is the *North*."

"Don't care where it is, them Bloker boys would stomp 'em to death in a minute. That's the one thing they can't stand. So naturally the Somerton boys wouldn't like it if we went back and forth 'cross the line."

It was like the game black kids in Somerton played when they were little. Not house or fairy tales, but a defiant line drawn with chalk: First one dares cross this got to fight *me*. The line was invisible now, but it was just as real. "So you stay with them just to keep them happy," she said.

Rosalinda's answer was quick and scornful. "Shoot, no. We know them white boys ain't gonna take us to the drugstore, or the movies, or a formal, or nowhere else except behind some bushes."

"You don't have to go in the bushes with a boy if you don't want to," Carlie argued, if only because it sounded like her mother's warnings, and lately she was in a mood to challenge all of her parents' statements. "Besides, I've got news for you. Paul asked me to the junior formal."

Rosalinda stared. "Well, if you go with him, you a bigger fool than I thought."

With a flip of her short skirt, she was gone, leaving Carlie's main question unanswered. All right, stick together if you want. But why, why do you have to stay in that dinky little *corner*?

Of course she wouldn't go to the dance with Paul.

He was not her kind either; her parents had been emphatic about that, too. Sometimes she tried to picture the ones who were, but she always failed. If they existed, which she doubted, they had vague faces belonging to no particular races, and they lived, like herself, in limbo.

Avoiding the gym, leaving by a side door, she tried to imagine what her family would do and say if she brought Paul home, and managed to laugh. Watching them throw him out would probably be very funny—to an outsider.

Some of the black boys from Somerton were on the bus, sweaty and excited after track practice. "Hi," she said, trying to detect whether they had become hostile. "Hi," they said, and went back to their soft easy talk. She remembered the anonymous taunt, and knew it had spread to the entire crowd.

Now you're in no man's land. When you break the big rules, you don't belong anywhere. You're an outlaw.

She walked home slowly, wandering aimlessly through fields. You've always been an outlaw. Ninth grade. She could still hear Miss Florence's warm drawl. "Honey, I sure wish you could find me somebody to help out with my laundry." And the two-edged satisfaction of the stock reply, "Yes, I know, isn't the servant problem awful? My mother's looking too." Only she had carried it too far, adding, "We had a wonderful Irish laundress last year, but her family moved away. We're looking for someone else just like her." That had overdone it, she knew, seeing the mixture of disbelief and indignation on the pretty little Southern teacher's face.

Outlaw. Refusing to sit in the *de facto* segregated balcony of the Duchess with the other black kids. Demanding a downstairs ticket every Saturday because her outlaw mother, who refused to accept segregation in any form, had ordered her to. Finding herself always alone after Rosalinda had tried to stick it out with her once, then fled after ten tense minutes to her friends upstairs. Deciding, finally, that she didn't particularly like movies and preferred to stay home and read a good book every Saturday.

Outlaw. Censoring all the books in the library. It was her idea, and Rosalinda had been reluctant at first, but soon she warmed to Carlie's daring and joined in with delight. It was Rosalinda who'd found the novel by Conrad, and together they'd censored every page, crossing out the ugly word in the title and the text, substituting a heavily capitalized proper noun in bright red pencil. "Here's another one, look here! Let *me* do it!" Rosalinda had squealed, snatching the pencil from Carlie's hand. "Thanks, cuddy. You're my cut-buddy." For once, Carlie hadn't minded not knowing how to talk like the others. She rolled the odd, condensed words silently on her tongue; she'd try them out in front of the mirror at home. "Shoot, the pencil's broke, that's all she wrote. Go steal one of Miss O'Shea's!" As Carlie heard herself giggling —a delicious new sound—she wondered, "Is this the way the others feel all the time?"

Then Miss O'Shea, the librarian, had come up silently behind them and taken the book away. "Have you read

this book, Carlotta?" was all she said. Months later Carlie
had wanted to and had gone back to look for it, but it was
not there. Some other outlaw must have done away with
it completely.

She was home now. Out of the school clothes and into
jeans. She folded her mauve sweater carefully and put it
away, running her hand over the soft textures that shim-
mered in the drawer. She hung her skirt in the closet beside the other skirts and slacks, all nicely tailored, expen-
sive. These are the things I like to wear every day. Why?
For myself, she answered fiercely. Hilda Hammer wears
hand-knit sweaters too. They all do. But sometimes
they're downright sloppy, and *they* get away with it.

Stepping into jeans, she saw Hilda's face, a mask of in-
nocence, turning to her in class. "Have you ever gone
out with Jackie Jamison?" Big, tongue-tied Jackie had
just finished fumbling through an easy algebra problem at
the board. Without thinking she had phrased her answer.
"No, Hilda. Have you?"

Well, you're in it now. For fair. Carlie shrugged and
held her head high again as she went downstairs. She still
had Walter Conley to take her to the junior formal. Walter, son of a fourth-generation mulatto family from North
Carolina who had kept the strain pure by careful inbreed-
ing with the other six mulatto families of Millersville,
eighteen miles away. Her parents approved of Walter as
much as they disapproved of nearly everyone else in the
world, everyone who was definitely either black or white.
He was conceited and not very bright, like all the Millers-

ville people, and Carlie's feelings about him were luke-warm at best, but his hair was yellow, his eyes blue, his nose Grecian, his skin like milk. Everyone would wonder and stare, and she would enjoy their confusion and never, never explain.

Downstairs in the quiet house, she hesitated, then tip-toed out the kitchen door and ran to her favorite part of the garden, the one spot her mother had never been able to tame. Here weeds and wild daisies grew riotous and free. She kicked off her shoes, shivering with pleasure as the warm tongues of grass caressed her bare feet. Rosa-linda had kicked and turned in one movement—like this!

"Carlotta!" her mother's voice called sharply from the house.

Carlie scrambled guiltily into her shoes. Her parents disapproved of that kind of dancing. But someday she would speak with the black kids' easy voices, and move with their knowing grace. In a place like this, where the sun was warm, and there were no fences to raise your pride against.

It would happen next year, she told herself as she trudged back to the house. When she entered the college her parents had promised her as a reward for enduring these four lonely years. One of those beautiful Shangri-la colleges down South, a walled-in paradise where you could live and laugh and forget the world outside.

But lately they had begun to renege on that promise, thrusting Vassar and Radcliffe catalogues into her hands whenever she mentioned Fisk or Howard. She realized they had never really meant it. She would hold them to it, though. She *would*.

With this to sustain her all through a week of avoiding the other students in the halls, of speaking only when spoken to in classes, it was hard to understand why she made her way down to the gym again at lunchtime. She had been determined to stay away, but the thunder of the music tempted her as she passed in the hall. Deliberately she turned instead and walked in to the edge of the brightly lit oval where the couples were dancing.

A moment later she was sorry. Paul rushed up to her and asked her to dance again. She hung back, trying to tell him why she couldn't.

"Come on," he said, almost dragging her out on the floor. She trembled, feeling three hundred eyes on her, then pulled herself together. Head high, Carlie. Isn't this what you wanted? He was holding her rather awkwardly, at arm's length. They moved jerkily around the floor. Then she heard his stiff voice, coming from far above her. "I know why you ran away last week, and I want to help you."

Like it's his duty. She shivered. She was glad when the dance was over and he had mumbled an excuse and disappeared into the crowd. I don't think I want anybody helping me. You're nice, but if you want to dance with me, that's one thing. If you want to help me, that's something else. Charity. *Run.* Now she wanted more than anything to be home in her own bed, hiding under the covers.

But she had started this thing; she had to see it through. And Zip DeMarco, a fiendish grin on his hideous, pimpled face, was inviting her to dance.

Zip, the class comedian. Teller of jokes and singer of off-color songs, imitator of Dean Martin and Don Rickles and a dozen assorted barnyard animals, wearer of false noses and moustaches and huge imitation false teeth. The Big Laugh.

As he led her out on the floor, she looked over her shoulder and saw Paul asking Rosalinda to dance—little ebony Rosalinda, with her wad of gum and her flying hoop earrings and her flashing smile. Carlie saw her shake her head, laugh, turn her back on him, and walk away. *Good for you*, she said silently without knowing why. Then she had no more time to watch or think. Out on the floor, moving to a fast, rollicking beat, the Zippo was true to form.

He shook his head and waggled his hips in imitation of the young black dancers he had seen on television. He threw her out in extravagant circles and jerked her violently back to him. He bent his knees and waddled. He threw back his head and howled. Then he released her hands, stepped back several feet, clapped his hands and shouted, "Boogaloo, girl!" A circle of handclapping spectators was beginning to form around them. She stood there woodenly, watching as he hunched his shoulders forward, wagging his head, rolling his eyes, wobbling his knees in a shuffle.

Zip's hard little eyes dared her, taunted her. From the

corner, laughing voices seemed to mock. And Carlie took the challenge. Release suddenly flowing through her limbs like honey, she snapped back her head and began to dance as she had never danced before, as she had seen the Somerton couples dance in rare moments of exhilaration or despair at the cellar parties long past midnight. Arms flung above her head, pelvis thrust forward, she began, bobbing and jerking and shaking suggestively. As he drew near her in clumsy enthusiastic imitation, she turned her back and pranced away, rolling her hips in vulgar exaggerated circles. "Do it, girl," Zip shouted. "Do your thing!" The all-white circle of spectators pressed closer and roared appreciation.

A short barking laugh burst from her as she turned to face him. Arms flailing, fingers snapping, she moved in teasing undulations, retreating backward, never allowing him to touch her. Then as the music rose to a crescendo, she arched her back and bent from the knees, still snapping her fingers.

Unable to restrain himself any longer, Zip lunged, grabbed her waist with thick, bruising fingers, and pulled her toward him. Carlie was struggling unsuccessfully to free herself when another attack came from behind—a female one, judging by the sharp nails that ripped through her sweater to her skin.

Carlie managed to twist her head and recognize her adversary—a braless witch with dark-painted eyes called Gina, who was screeching like a bluejay and striking out blindly at both of them. Zip actually had a girlfriend.

He had to release Carlie to fend Gina off. Carlie's instinctive strategy, to disappear, proved best. She slid down toward the floor while the couple clashed above her. Other whites joined the battle. Carlie tried to make herself invisible in the old, childish way, by closing her eyes and invoking the magic formula: *If I can't see them, they can't see me.* She made herself smaller, too, curling into a ball for protection against stray kicks and trampling. She could not tell how many were fighting above her, but the clamor sounded as if she had provoked enough rage to trigger World War Three.

The music's insane pounding ended abruptly, and, with it, the war. A voice of authority came over the PA system instead, restoring order. But Carlie still lay there with her knees drawn up, her eyes tightly closed, and her head jerking spasmodically to the beat of the dead music.

Hands tried to make her get up, and failed. Strong arms lifted her firmly to her feet in spite of her struggles.

"Don't fight us, baby," an easy voice said. "We won't let you fall."

She opened her eyes. It was Jackie Jamison, supporting her on her left side, and Teddy Harper with a firm grip on her right. It was all of them, come out of the corner at last to surround her with safety-in-numbers.

Little Harvey said from the sidelines, "You sure picked the hard way to show us you could dance, gal."

"It was worth it," she whispered, leaning gratefully against Teddy.

"Well," Teddy said, "don't go wasting your talents no more, hear?"

"Later for that," said Rosalinda. "Let's get Carlie home."

She started to protest that she didn't *want* to go home. Then she saw where they were leading her. To the most desirable place in the world, the only place she ever wanted to be.

The corner.

You Rap, I'll Reap

My used-to-be best friend Sheilah thinks she's some smart. Always rapping about the capitalist this and the racist that. And about how her bush is bigger than my bush, and she's blacker than I am. Even though she's really Gulden's Spicy Brown Mustard color while my complexion is like Yuban Coffee in the jar.

Sheilah said I was dumb for not knowing how black you are means how black you think, how black you are inside. And how, being so backward and all, I really needed somebody like her to hip me. Well, she hipped me, all right, but maybe not in the way she intended.

We got to fight the Man's system because it exploits us, Sheilah says. In the meantime we got to get our own socialist system among ourselves. I may not have known all those big words before I met Sheilah, but I know what she means. Share what you got. Or, you help me, I help you.

Well all right, I tell her, I dig it, that's the way we live in the projects anyway. And it ain't no big thing.

Take last week when old Mrs. Dawkins across the hall

was late getting her check. I borrowed ten dollars toward
her rent from Mrs. Stevens, the lady I work for after
school. Mrs. Dawkins got the rest from Lola, the new girl
my age down the hall who has a baby, and from Po Boy,
the numbers writer, and Madame James, the card reader,
and Pork Chop, who runs the newsstand on the corner.
Then her check finally came, so on Sunday she cooked a
big dinner, ham and fried chicken and yams and corn-
bread and greens, and invited everybody in the building
who'd helped her make her rent.

Sheilah, who lives downstairs, wasn't there. Maybe that
was why we had such a good time.

Course, Mrs. Dawkins couldn't pay us back right away,
not after buying all that food. We didn't ask her to. How
could we, when she'd been so nice to us? We don't exactly keep books on each other in the projects, but it all
works out somehow. Mrs. Dawkins, now, she does favors
for everybody. At the party she offered to keep Lola's
baby any time she couldn't pay a sitter. And she lets *me*
stay over her place any time I want.

I stayed with Mrs. Dawkins two whole months one
time. My Aunt Lou and her two daughters had come up
from down South and had no place to go. I didn't mind
giving them my room. Them cousins of mine talk too
much anyway. Over Mrs. Dawkins' I can do anything I
want, study and read in peace and quiet or stay up all
night and watch TV.

A boss time was had by all till late Sunday night, but
Monday morning was blue, just like the song. I had for-
gotten all about no longer having five dollars to get my

school dresses out of the cleaners. And I hadn't washed and ironed all weekend. I had nothing to wear to school. I was desperate. Mom won't let me leave the house unless I'm neat and clean.

Finally I went down the hall and knocked on Lola's door and asked to borrow a dress. I had just met her the night before, but I thought she was real nice and might say yes. She did. She also said she was just as broke as I was from helping out Mrs. Dawkins, so all four of our feet were on the ground. Not barefoot, which is what they mean when they say it down South where they are *really* poor. Just walking to save carfare.

Walking together, the twelve blocks didn't seem so long, and by the time we got to school I had a new best friend.

But who should we run into when we got there but Sheilah, getting dropped off by her boyfriend Jomo in his white Jaguar. And she was *togged* too, in a new tangerine dress that was so bright it almost blinded me. To tell the truth, it didn't become her, but I'd never say it to her face.

"Sheilah," I say, "how about letting me have back that blue skirt I loaned you?"

"Oh, I can't," she says, "because I loaned it to one of the sisters who had nothing to wear."

"You loaned my skirt to somebody else?" I cried.

"Of course," she said. "We brothers and sisters have to help one another. It's the only way we can survive in this rotten system."

"True, true," says Lola, like she's in church. I could tell

she was impressed by Sheilah's jive. But then, she'd never heard it before.

Sheilah looks at Lola with interest. "Introduce me to your new friend, Gloria dear," she says. So I did. But Lola backed away. She is kind of shy around people who talk better than she does.

"Well, look," I say to Sheilah, "how about lending me that green jumper of yours to wear to school this week, till I get my stuff out of the cleaners?"

"Gloria, honey," Sheilah says, "you know you're my sister, and I'd do anything in the world for you. But this rag I've got on is the only thing left in my closet. I gave all my other clothes to the sisters in the Movement. Besides, we're not the same size."

Which is a barefaced lie. That Sheilah has worn everything I ever owned.

"At least," Sheilah goes on, "*you* have a job." And she looks at me like I should be ashamed of working. "You can buy all the lovely clothes you want. I was about to ask you when you are going to stop being so selfish and donate a little something to the cause."

Fortunately the second bell rang then and we had to go in, so I didn't get a chance to call that girl the name I had in mind.

Then at lunchtime, here she comes busting in the cafeteria just when Lola and I were counting our money. We were making up our minds whether to have a whole bologna sandwich apiece or share a roast beef one. My mouth was all set for that roast beef. Then it turns out that the donation Sheilah had in mind was for me to buy her lunches.

"Gloria darling," she says, "you know I devote all my time to the Movement. I can't earn money like you do. My time is too valuable."

Now, why didn't the girl just come straight out and say she was hungry? I could dig that. But no, she had to tell me I'm selfish for working, and it's my *duty* to feed her because she's a better person than I am.

Her tongue was hanging out so far it was ready to lick gravy off the floor, though. She spose to be my best friend. I couldn't very well let her starve. I bought *three* bologna sandwiches.

So, after school, there was nothing to do but ask Mrs. Stevens to loan me another ten dollars.

"You can take it out of my salary this week," I told her.

"Gloria," Mrs. Stevens said, "you will then owe me *more* than your salary."

"I know that," I say, and I can't explain why I'm mad.

Mrs. Stevens pays me three dollars a day to pick up her babies, Mike Jr. and Molly, at the nursery school and keep them till she gets home from work at 5:30. I'm sposed to straighten up the house and start supper too, but only if I have time. The babies are nice, and the pay ain't bad, especially since Mrs. Stevens is so easy to work for. I know all that as well as she does.

But there's a lot she *don't* know, because she's white, and I ain't about to tell her.

And now she really pulls her whiteness on me. "Well, I have obligations, too," she begins in that talking-down way I can't stand, whether it comes from her or Sheilah. "I have to meet my bills every week. I don't know why *you* people can't be more responsible. What happened to the other ten dollars, Gloria?"

"I had to help out a friend," I mumbled. Did she really think I was going to tell her all the details about the way we have to live? I don't know why, but people like Mrs. Stevens have a way of making you shamed of it even when it's not your fault.

"Well," she says, "maybe some of these people aren't *really* your friends."

That did start me thinking. I still wasn't about to tell her all my business, though.

But Mrs. Stevens always makes you bring things right down front. She calls it "being straightforward." "Why do you need another ten so soon?" she wants to know.

So I had to explain about needing five dollars to get my school dresses out of the cleaners. Plus another five for my lunches and carfare. I didn't say nothing about Lola or Sheilah or Mrs. Dawkins, though. Mrs. Stevens wouldn't understand.

"Well," she says firmly, "I'm sorry. But five dollars is all I can let you have, Gloria. That will buy your lunches and get you to school. And it will also keep you from owing me more than one week's salary."

Then she sighs. "But I guess you *do* have to have something to wear."

Mrs. Stevens is not really a bad lady, not at all. She looks at me and sighs again. "And I suppose we *are* about the same size."

Of course we are, perfect nines, cause I've hung her clothes up plenty of times. Tried 'em on too. But I'm proud to say I never borrowed any.

Mrs. Stevens opens her closet and starts handing me things. "Take this. And this. And this." All-a-time mumbling things about "planning" and "budgeting" and "responsibility." Every time she says something like this, she hands me another dress. Like she's paying me for listening. See, she's trying to teach me sense, but she's putting me down too, and she knows it. So she keeps giving me more.

She winds up with a little lecture about how I'll have to alter them myself. If I haven't learned to sew yet, it's time I did. I should also wash and iron my things if I can't afford the cleaners. And so forth, and so on, and blah, blah, blah.

Then she hands me a *tough* blue and yellow three-piece suit my mouth has been watering for ever since I first saw it on her. I leave with that and six dresses. Not bad.

Only that night I have to listen to some of *Sheilah's* lectures, too, and hers don't pay me, they cost me.

The way it happens is this. Lola and me are in her apartment, trying on Mrs. Stevens' dresses. We're letting out seams on the ones I'm giving Lola when Sheilah busts in.

"Oh! Gloria! I didn't know you'd be here!" she cries.

I guess not, since she's wearing the green jumper she told me she didn't have anymore. I didn't mention it, though. Just listened while she came on with jive about how Lola should stop staying home and being selfish and come out to Movement meetings. Lola didn't answer and neither did I. We just kept on trying on them dresses, till Sheilah couldn't stand it no more.

"Where," she asks, "did you get all those lovely clothes?"

"From the lady she works for," Lola said.

"That's nice," Sheilah said. "Of course, I never get things like these. I'm too proud to beg from white folks."

How I kept the cuss words down my throat I'll never know.

"But somebody has to do it, I suppose," she goes on. "We have to take things from Miss Ann and Mr. Charlie every chance we get. And then we have to share them among ourselves."

"Uh-huh," I say.

"This three-piece suit," purrs Sheilah, taking it up, "will just about fit me."

"Oh, no, it won't, Sheilah *darling*," I tell her. "We're not the same size. Remember?"

Well, Sheilah really did her number then. She called me bourgeois capitalist and selfish individualist and Uncle Tom and Aunt Jemima and every other name in her book. She called me everything but a female dog, which was what I was about to call her.

And I would have too, if Lola hadn't spoke up quietly

and asked Sheilah to leave, because her noise had already woke up the baby and might soon get Lola put out of her apartment.

Took me a half hour to calm down after that. The perfect way that blue and yellow suit fitted helped a lot. I strutted around in it, rehearsing what I would tell Sheilah tomorrow in between bites of my roast beef sandwich.

"You rap, Sheilah darling, and I'll reap. And I'll share my harvest with anybody I please, except you, cause you done finally rapped yourself out of my reapings. You have really torn your drawers this time and you won't get another pair from me. And you can call that any name you want—capitalism, Tomism, selfism, or dogism—cause I done spotted your game and I can call it by the same name."

All Around the Mulberry Tree

When we first came up here from Wrightsville, Georgia, I thought I'd like living in the Franklin Delano Roosevelt Projects. After all, my name is Roosevelt too. Roosevelt Green. With a name like that I could pretend the whole place was mine.

Turns out, not even one corner of our apartment belongs to us. It's impossible to live there the way normal people do in a normal place like Wrightsville.

I thought being twelve stories up in the air would make me feel free, like a bird. And great, like the King of the Mountain. But living high brings me down. Cause every time you put one foot in front of the other, you break a rule.

There's a rule for everything in the projects. Times to put out your trash. Times and places to do your laundry. No running up and down stairs. Everyone under sixteen inside by nine o'clock. Just like jail.

The projects even have a warden, who is called the Superintendent. And each building has a spy who reports to him. The spy gets free rent for snooping and ratting on the other tenants. Mostly you never know who the spy in your building is. But we found out pretty quick that ours was Mrs. Broadnax.

Mrs. Broadnax is a skinny old widow lady with silver-rimmed dark glasses and two gold front teeth and a sly, crooked smile. She always has a hat on. I don't know where she finds them ugly hats. I don't know where she got them glasses, either. They're the darkest I ever seen. But they help her by hiding her eyes. She never looks straight at you when she's talking to you because she's too busy writing up the report in her head.

The trouble with Mrs. Broadnax started because Mom wanted to talk to her friend Mrs. Gaddie. Mrs. Gaddie lives right under us in 11-A. She is from Georgia too. Her home is in Waycross, which is a long way from Wrightsville. But up here, the hundred miles between our home towns seems a lot closer than the one floor between our apartments.

Every day when Mom was ready to talk, she would bang a broom handle on the floor. Back would come a knocking from below. One knock meant, "No, I'm too busy now." Two knocks meant, "Yes, let's have a visit."

If there were two knocks Mom would stick her head out the window and yell down, "How you feelin' today, Essie?"

And Mrs. Gaddie would stick her head out and answer, "No use in complainin', Rosine."

And they would go on like that till they ran out of

things to talk about. Or till one of them decided she had something else to do.

One of the things they rapped about a lot was the misery of living in the projects and always finding out you broke some rule. And what they would do to the person who was ratting on them if they ever found out who it was.

I guess that's why Mrs. Broadnax about had a fit when she walked by and heard them. Or else she was just jealous because she didn't have a friend.

Anyway, in five minutes she was knocking on our door.

"Mrs. Green," she said, "you simply cannot hang out of your window like that. If you keep on doing it, you and your family will have to move."

"What are people supposed to do up here?" Mom complained. "This place don't have no front stoops to sit on. And no back porches, either. How's a person going to be sociable?"

"Visit your friend in her apartment," Mrs. Broadnax said.

"I can't go down there and leave these children," Mom said. She wasn't talking about my brother Cephas and me. We're big enough to take care of ourselves. She meant Carmen and Larisse, who are two and four.

"Invite her up here, then."

"She can't come. Her babies are even smaller than mine."

"I don't know what to suggest, then."

"Well, *I* do. I suggest you take yourself out of my

apartment and mind your own business."

Mrs. Broadnax did just that. But she knew she had won.

We knew it, too. It was clear Mrs. Broadnax was a big shot in the projects. It had to be her who had caused all those notes from the Superintendent to appear in our mailbox. Telling us to get rid of our cat because pets weren't allowed. Making Cephas take his school art-work down from our front door. Warning us not to play records with the door open, even on a hot night when we needed air.

Dad had been against Mrs. Broadnax and on our side all those other times. But he wasn't much help in this.

"She's right," he told Mom when he got home. "I don't want you falling out that window and breaking your neck. If you have to see Essie Gaddie, go to her apart-ment. You can send the children outdoors."

And he went back to eating his watermelon. I guess he felt he had a right to enjoy it in peace, after lugging it up the whole twelve flights of stairs because the elevator was broken again. It was the first watermelon we'd had since we came up North. Getting it home was such hard work, I figured it might be the last.

I saved some seeds and slipped them in my pocket. I planned to put them with my other souvenirs of home: the palmetto leaf, the piece of sugar cane, the hairs from our horse Nellie's tail, the peach pits and pecans from the trees in our yard. I keep these things to help me remember how good life was down home, even though Daddy wasn't making no money there.

The next day, Mom didn't bang on the floor as usual.

Nor did she stick her head out the window.

Instead, she told us, "You Roosevelt, you Cephas, take your sisters outside and play with them. Don't let them out of your sight. I'm going down to visit Mrs. Gaddie."

We were happy. That little patch of ground behind our building wasn't even big enough for Nellie to lie down on. But at least it was *ground*, and grass was coming up on it. And right in the center of the grass was a little mulberry tree just turning green.

Living in the city with all its concrete, you forget to notice when winter is over and it is spring. Now we had noticed, and we felt like celebrating. First we took off our shoes. Man! but that grass felt good under our bare feet. Then I took my sisters' hands and led them to the tree. We skipped around it, singing:

All around the mulberry tree,
The monkey chases the weasel.

We had just about forgot we were in the city when that mean old Mrs. Broadnax came by. In her blue coat and hat she looked just like a cop.

"Children, what are you doing? Don't you see that 'Keep Off the Grass' sign? Get away from there!"

Carmen and Larisse went on skipping and singing, "The monkey chases the weasel."

"*You* are the monkeys," Mrs. Broadnax said. "You come up here from the country and act just like animals."

"You ain't our mother," I told her.

"No, but I can talk to her," Mrs. Broadnax said. "And I will."

And sure enough, she did, later on that day.

Mom was ready for her. "What you mean, calling my children monkeys and animals?"

"They have no respect for property," Mrs. Broadnax said. "That lawn has just been planted. It is not for anybody to walk on. It is for everybody to look at and enjoy."

"That ain't what it's for where *I* come from," Mom told her. "Where I come from, the earth is for people to use. And running and jumping on it is the healthiest thing children can do."

"Well, you're not down there any more. You're in the city now," Mrs. Broadnax said.

"Yes, and what's wrong with it is too many people like you. Give you people a little job, a little money, and you think you own the earth. Next thing you know we'll have to ask your permission to breathe."

"Don't say you weren't warned," Mrs. Broadnax said.

"I won't," said Mom. But I think she was sick of Mrs. Broadnax and her rules, because the next day she sent us outside again without a word about what we could or couldn't do.

Larisse and Carmen had brought spoons this time. They had a lot of fun digging in the ground while me and Cephas climbed the tree.

Then Larisse called us down. "Let's pretend we planting a garden," she cried, waving her spoon. Larisse is old enough to remember our fields down home.

I pulled the watermelon seeds out of my pocket. There

were eight of them. Larisse and Carmen had dug six holes around the tree. I dropped a seed in each hole and still had two left over for my collection.

We covered the seeds with dirt. Then we went back to climbing the tree—all of us except Carmen, cause she's too little. But when all three of us got on the same limb, it snapped.

We wasn't hurt. It was such a little tree, we didn't have far to fall. But when we got up from the grass and brushed ourselves off there was Mrs. Broadnax watching us— not saying a word, just smiling her sneaky little smile.

That night when Dad got home from work he found a note from the Superintendent in our mailbox. He would have to pay an eighty-dollar fine.

He waved the note at Mom. "It says here I have been warned not to let the kids tear up the lawn. What does it mean?"

"What it says," she said calmly. "That Broadnax bat-tle-ax came up here yesterday and said to keep the kids off the grass."

"And you let them play there again anyway?"

"I did," said Mom. "Nobody is going to tell me how to live any more. I got my own ideas on how to raise chil-dren."

"Well, have you got any ideas on how to raise eighty dollars?"

Mom was silent.

"I thought you didn't. I'm going to have to work my head off to get that money. But first I'm going to take it out of your hides. You first, Roosevelt."

It didn't hurt so bad when he beat me and Cephas. What hurt was hearing him threaten to beat Mom too. He told her if she wanted to be in the country so bad, she should go and find her a country man.

We were half afraid she would do just that. But, though she cried and moaned all night long, she didn't go nowhere.

It rained for more than a week. We couldn't have gone outdoors if we'd been allowed to.

Then there was a clear day. Cephas and I came home from school and decided to fool around outside for a while. We wandered around to the back of the building.

The little patch of grass had been trimmed, and the broken branch had been sawed off the tree so neatly you couldn't tell it had been there. There was a little wire fence around the tree and a bigger one around the grass. It looked neat and perfect and dead. Just like a graveyard. Only thing missing was tombstones.

Cephas spotted something. "Hey, Roosevelt! Look!" he cried.

I looked where his finger was pointing. Coming up around the base of the tree were some broad, wrinkled, light-green leaves.

My watermelon vines!

I guess maybe you never seen a watermelon vine, but it's one of the biggest plants in the world. It spreads out all over the place and travels anywhere there's space for it to go.

My vines are almost four feet long now. I water them every night in the hour between dark and curfew. And I tell them what I want them to do:

"First, crawl in Mrs. Broadnax's window and choke her.

"Then make it so people won't have to live high up in the sky any more. Make it so they can come down, and plant things, and walk around on the ground.

"Send your roots under this building, and crack the foundations, and make it come tumbling down."

When it happens, I'll be King of the Mountain, sitting on top of the ruins with a hunk of watermelon in each hand.

The Scribe

We been living in the apartment over the Silver Dollar Check Cashing Service five years. But I never had any reason to go in there till two days ago, when Mom had to go to the Wash-a-Mat and asked me to get some change.

And man! Are those people who come in there in some bad shape.

Old man Silver and old man Dollar, who own the place, have signs tacked up everywhere:

NO LOUNGING, NO LOITERING

THIS IS NOT A WAITING ROOM

and

MINIMUM CHECK CASHING FEE, 50¢

and

LETTERS ADDRESSED, 50¢

and

LETTERS READ, 75¢

and

LETTERS WRITTEN, ONE DOLLAR

And everybody who comes in there to cash a check gets their picture taken like they're some kind of criminal.

After I got my change, I stood around for a while digging the action. First comes an old lady with some kind of long form to fill out. The mean old man behind the counter points to the "One Dollar" sign. She nods. So he starts to fill it out for her.

"Name?"

"Muskogee Marie Lawson."

"SPELL it!" he hollers.

"M, m, u, s—well, I don't exactly know, sir."

"I'll put down 'Marie,' then. Age?"

"Sixty-three my last birthday."

"Date of birth?"

"March twenty-third"—a pause—"I think, 1900."

"Look, Marie," he says, which makes me mad, hearing him first-name a dignified old gray-haired lady like that, "if you'd been born in 1900, you'd be seventy-two. Either I put that down, or I put 1910."

"Whatever you think best, sir," she says timidly.

He sighs, rolls his eyes to the ceiling, and bangs his fist on the form angrily. Then he fills out the rest.

"One dollar," he says when he's finished. She pays like she's grateful to him for taking the trouble.

Next is a man with a cane, a veteran who has to let the government know he moved. He wants old man Silver to do this for him, but he doesn't want him to know he can't do it himself.

"My eyes are kind of bad, sir, will you fill this thing

out for me? Tell them I moved from 121 South 15th Street to 203 North Decatur Street."

Old man Silver doesn't blink an eye. Just fills out the form, and charges the crippled man a dollar.

And it goes on like that. People who can't read or write or count their change. People who don't know how to pay their gas bills, don't know how to fill out forms, don't know how to address envelopes. And old man Silver and old man Dollar cleaning up on all of them. It's pitiful. It's disgusting. Makes me so mad I want to yell.

And I do, but mostly at Mom. "Mom, did you know there are hundreds of people in this city who can't read and write?"

Mom isn't upset. She's a wise woman. "Of course, James," she says. "A lot of the older people around here haven't had your advantages. They came from down South, and they had to quit school very young to go to work.

"In the old days, nobody cared whether our people got an education. They were only interested in getting the crops in." She sighed. "Sometimes I think they *still* don't care. If we hadn't gotten you into that good school, you might not be able to read so well either. A lot of boys and girls your age can't, you know."

"But that's awful!" I say. "How do they expect us to make it in a big city? You can't even cross the streets if you can't read the WALK and DON'T WALK signs."

"It's hard," Mom says, "but the important thing to remember is it's no disgrace. There was a time in history when nobody could read or write except a special class of people."

And Mom takes down her Bible. She has three Bible study certificates and is always giving me lessons from Bible history. I don't exactly go for all the stuff she believes in, but sometimes it *is* interesting.

"In ancient times," she says, "no one could read or write except a special class of people known as *scribes*. It was their job to write down the laws given by the rabbis and the judges. No one else could do it.

"Jesus criticized the scribes," she goes on, "because they were so proud of themselves. But he needed them to write down his teachings."

"Man," I said when she finished, "that's something."

My mind was working double-time. I'm the best reader and writer in our class. Also it was summertime. I had nothing much to do except go to the park or hang around the library and read till my eyeballs were ready to fall out, and I was tired of doing both.

So the next morning, after my parents went to work, I took Mom's card table and a folding chair down to the sidewalk. I lettered a sign with a Magic Marker, and I was in business. My sign said:

PUBLIC SCRIBE—ALL SERVICES FREE

I set my table up in front of the Silver Dollar and waited for business. Only one thing bothered me. If the people couldn't read, how would they know what I was there for?

But five minutes had hardly passed when an old lady stopped and asked me to read her grandson's letter. She explained that she had just broken her glasses. I knew she was fibbing, but I kept quiet.

I read the grandson's letter. It said he was having a fine time in California, but was a little short. He would send her some money as soon as he made another payday. I handed the letter back to her.

"Thank you, son," she said, and gave me a quarter.

I handed that back to her too.

The word got around. By noontime I had a whole crowd of customers around my table. I was kept busy writing letters, addressing envelopes, filling out forms, and explaining official-looking letters that scared people half to death.

I didn't blame them. The language in some of those letters—"Establish whether your disability is one-fourth, one-third, one-half, or total, and substantiate in paragraph 3 (b) below"—would upset anybody. I mean, why can't the government write English like everybody else?

Most of my customers were old, but there were a few young ones too. Like the girl who had gotten a letter about her baby from the Health Service and didn't know what "immunization" meant.

At noontime one old lady brought me some iced tea and a peach, and another gave me some fried chicken wings. I was really having a good time, when the shade of all the people standing around me suddenly vanished. The sun hit me like a ton of hot bricks.

Only one long shadow fell across my table. The shadow of a tall, heavy, blue-eyed cop. In our neighborhood, when they see a cop, people scatter. That was why the back of my neck was burning.

"What are you trying to do here, sonny?" the cop asks.

"Help people out," I tell him calmly, though my knees are knocking together under the table.

"Well, you know," he says, "Mr. Silver and Mr. Dollar have been in business a long time on this corner. They are very respected men in this neighborhood. Are you trying to run them out of business?"

"I'm not charging anybody," I pointed out.

"That," the cop says, "is exactly what they don't like. Mr. Silver says he is glad to have some help with the letter-writing. Mr. Dollar says it's only a nuisance to them anyway and takes up too much time. But if you don't charge for your services, it's unfair competition."

Well, why not? I thought. After all, I could use a little profit.

"All right," I tell him. "I'll charge a quarter."

"Then it is my duty to warn you," the cop says, "that it's against the law to conduct a business without a license. The first time you accept a fee, I'll close you up and run you off this corner."

He really had me there. What did I know about licenses? I'm only thirteen, after all. Suddenly I didn't feel like the big black businessman anymore. I felt like a little kid who wanted to holler for his mother. But she was at work, and so was Daddy.

"I'll leave," I said, and did, with all the cool I could muster. But inside I was burning up, and not from the sun.

One little old lady hollered "You big bully!" and shook her umbrella at the cop. But the rest of those people were so beaten-down they didn't say anything. Just shuffled back on inside to give Mr. Silver and Mr. Dollar their hard-earned money like they always did.

I was so mad I didn't know what to do with myself that afternoon. I couldn't watch TV. It was all soap operas anyway, and they seemed dumber than ever. The library didn't appeal to me either. It's not air-conditioned, and the day was hot and muggy.

Finally I went to the park and threw stones at the swans in the lake. I was careful not to hit them, but they made good targets because they were so fat and white. Then after a while the sun got lower. I kind of cooled off and came to my senses. They were just big, dumb, beautiful birds, and not my enemies. I threw them some crumbs from my sandwich and went home.

"Daddy," I asked that night, "how come you and Mom never cash checks downstairs in the Silver Dollar?"

"Because," he said, "we have an account at the bank, where they cash our checks free."

"Well, why doesn't everybody do that?" I wanted to know.

"Because some people want all their money right away," he said. "The bank insists that you leave them a minimum balance."

"How much?" I asked him.

"Only five dollars."

"But that five dollars still belongs to you after you leave it there?"

"Sure," he says. "And if it's in a savings account, it earns interest."

"So why can't people see they lose money when they *pay* to have their checks cashed?"

"A lot of *our* people," Mom said, "are scared of banks, period. Some of them remember the Depression, when all the banks closed and the people couldn't get their money out. And others think banks are only for white people. They think they'll be insulted, or maybe even arrested, if they go in there."

Wow. The more I learned, the more pitiful it was. "Are there any black people working at our bank?"

"There didn't used to be," Mom said, "but now they have Mr. Lovejoy and Mrs. Adams. You know Mrs. Adams, she's nice. She has a daughter your age."

"Hmmm," I said, and shut up before my folks started to wonder why I was asking all those questions.

The next morning, when the Silver Dollar opened, I was right there. I hung around near the door, pretending to read a copy of *Jet* magazine.

"Psst," I said to each person who came in. "I know where you can cash checks *free.*"

It wasn't easy convincing them. A man with a wine bottle in a paper bag blinked his red eyes at me like he didn't believe he had heard right. A carpenter with tools hanging all around his belt said he was on his lunch hour and didn't have time. And a big fat lady with two shopping bags pushed past me and almost knocked me down, she was in such a hurry to give Mr. Silver and Mr. Dollar her money.

But finally I had a little group who were interested. It wasn't much. Just three people. Two men—one young, one old—and the little old lady who'd asked me to read her the letter from California. Seemed the grandson had made his payday and sent her a money order.

"How far is this place?" asked the young man.

"Not far. Just six blocks," I told him.

"Aw shoot. I ain't walking all that way just to save fifty cents."

So then I only had two. I was careful not to tell them where we were going. When we finally got to the Establishment Trust National Bank, I said, "This is the place."

"I ain't goin' in there," said the old man. "No sir. Not me. You ain't gettin' me in *there*." And he walked away quickly, going back in the direction we had come.

To tell the truth, the bank did look kind of scary. It was a big building with tall white marble pillars. A lot of Brink's armored trucks and Cadillacs were parked out front. Uniformed guards walked back and forth inside with guns. It might as well have had a "Colored Keep Out" sign.

Whereas the Silver Dollar is small and dark and funky and dirty. It has trash on the floors and tape across the broken windows. People going in there feel right at home.

I looked at the little old lady. She smiled back bravely.

"Well, we've come this far, son," she said. "Let's not turn back now."

So I took her inside. Fortunately Mrs. Adams' window was near the front.

"Hi, James," she said.

"I've brought you a customer," I told her.

Mrs. Adams took the old lady to a desk to fill out some forms. They were gone a long time, but finally they came back.

"Now, when you have more business with the bank, Mrs. Franklin, just bring it to me," Mrs. Adams said.

"I'll do that," the old lady said. She held out her shiny new bankbook. "Son, do me a favor and read that to me."

"Mrs. Minnie Franklin," I read aloud. "July 9, 1972. Thirty-seven dollars."

"That sounds real nice," Mrs. Franklin said. "I guess now I have a bankbook, I'll have to get me some glasses."

Mrs. Adams winked at me over the old lady's head, and I winked back.

"Do you want me to walk you home?" I asked Mrs. Franklin.

"No thank you, son," she said. "I can cross streets by myself all right. I know red from green."

And then she winked at both of us, letting us know she knew what was happening.

"Son," she went on, "don't ever be afraid to try a thing just because you've never done it before. I took a bus up here from Alabama by myself forty-four years ago. I ain't thought once about going back. But I've stayed too long in one neighborhood since I've been in this city. Now I think I'll go out and take a look at *this* part of town."

Then she was gone. But she had really started me thinking. If an old lady like that wasn't afraid to go in a bank and open an account for the first time in her life, why should *I* be afraid to go up to City Hall and apply for a license?

Wonder how much they charge you to be a scribe?

Mom Luby and the Social Worker

Puddin' and I been livin' with Mom Luby three years, ever since our mother died. We like it fine. But when Mom Luby took us down to the Welfare, we thought our happy days were over and our troubles about to begin.

"Chirren," she said that day, "I got to get some of this State Aid so I can give you everything you need. Shoes for you, Elijah, and dresses for Puddin' now she's startin' school. And lunch money and carfare and stuff like that. But the only way I can get it is to say I'm your mother. So don't mess up my lie."

Mom Luby is old as Santa Claus, maybe older, with hair like white cotton and false teeth that hurt so much she takes them out and gums her food. But she's strong as a young woman and twice as proud. Much too proud to say she's our grandmother, which is something the Welfare people might believe.

So we went down there scared that morning, Puddin' holding tight onto both our hands. But we was lucky. The lady behind the desk didn't even look at us, and we got out of that gloomy old State Building safe and free.

Man! Was I glad to get back to Division Street where people don't ask questions about your business.

When we got home, a whole bunch of people was waiting for Mom to let them in the speakeasy she runs in the back room. Jake was there, and Sissiemae, and Bobo and Walter and Lucas and Mose and Zerline. They are regular customers who come every evening to drink the corn liquor Mom gets from down South and eat the food she fixes, gumbo and chicken wings and ribs and potato salad and greens.

Bobo picked Puddin' up to see how much she weighed (a lot), until she hollered to be let down. Jake gave me a quarter to take his shoes down to Gumby's Fantastic Shoe Shine Parlor and get them shined and keep the change. We let the people in the front door and through the red curtain that divides the front room from the back. Soon they were settled around the big old round table with a half-gallon jar of corn. Then Sissiemae and Lucas wanted chicken wings, and I had to collect the money while Mom heated them up on the stove. There was so much to do, I didn't pay no attention to the tapping on the front door.

But then it came again, louder, like a woodpecker working on a tree.

"Elijah," Mom says, "run see who it is trying to chip a hole in that door. If it be the police, tell them I'll see them Saturday."

But it wasn't the cops, who come around every Saturday night to get their money and drink some of Mom's corn and put their big black shoes up on the table. It was a little brownskin lady with straightened hair and glasses and black high-top shoes. She carried a big leather envelope and was dressed all in dark blue.

"Good afternoon," she says. "I am Miss Rushmore of the Department of Child Welfare, Bureau of Family Assistance. Is Mrs. Luby at home?"

"I am she," says Mom. "Never been nobody else. Come in, honey, and set yourself down. Take off them shoes, they do look like real corn-crushers to me."

"No thank you," says Miss Rushmore. She sits on the edge of one of Mom's chairs and starts pulling papers out of the envelope. "This must be Elijah."

"Yes ma'am," I say.

"And where is Arlethia?"

"Taking her nap," says Mom, with a swat of the broom at the middle of the curtain, which Puddin' was peeking through. She's five and fat, and she loves to hang around grownups. Especially when they eating.

Mom hit the curtain with the broom again, and Puddin' ran off. The lady didn't even notice. She was too busy peeking under the lids of the pots on the stove.

"Salt pork and lima beans," she says. "Hardly a proper diet for growing children."

"Well," says Mom, "when I get me some of this State Aid, maybe I can afford to get them canned vegetables and box cereal. Meanwhile you welcome to what we have."

The lady acted like she didn't hear that. She just wrinkled up her nose like she smelled something bad.

"First," she says, "we must have a little talk about your budget. Do you understand the importance of financial planning?"

"Man arranges and God changes," says Mom. "When I got it, I spends it, when I don't, I do without."

"That," says the lady, "is precisely the attitude I am here to correct." She pulls out a big yellow sheet of paper. "Now this is our Family Budget Work Sheet. What is your rent?"

"I ain't paid it in so long I forgot," Mom says. Which set me in a fit because everybody but this dumb lady knows Mom owns the house. Behind her back Mom gave me a whack that stopped my giggles.

The lady sighed. "We'll get to the budget later," she says. "First, there are some questions you left blank today. How old were you when Elijah was born?"

"Thirty-two," says Mom.

"And he is now thirteen, which would make you forty-five," says the lady.

"Thirty-eight," says Mom without batting an eye.

"I'll put down forty-five," says the lady, giving Mom a funny look. "No doubt your hard life has aged you beyond your years. Now, who is the father, and where is he?"

"Lemme see," says Mom, twisting a piece of her hair. "I ain't seen Mr. Luby since 1942. He was a railroad man, you see, and one time he just took a train out of here and never rode back."

"1942," Miss Rushmore wrote on the paper. And then said, "But that's impossible!"

"The dear Lord do teach us," says Mom, "that nothing in life is impossible if we just believe enough."

"Hey, Mom, we're out of corn!" cries Lucas from the back room.

Miss Rushmore looked very upset. "Why," she says, "you've got a man in there."

"Sure do sound like it, don't it?" Mom says. "Sure do. You got one too, honey?"

"That's my business," says the lady.

"I was just trying to be sociable," says Mom pleasantly. "You sure do seem interested in mine."

I ran back there and fetched another mason jar of corn from the shed kitchen. I told Lucas and Bobo and them to be quiet. Which wasn't going to be easy, cause them folks get good and loud when they get in a card game. I also dragged Puddin' away from the potato salad bowl, where she had stuck both her hands, and brought her in the front room with me. She was bawling. The lady gave her a weak smile.

"Now," Mom says. "About these shoes and school clothes."

"I am not sure," Miss Rushmore says, "that you can get them. There is something wrong in this house that I have not yet put my finger on. But this is what you do. First you fill out Form 905, which you get at the Bureau of Family Assistance, room 1203. Then you call the Division of Child Welfare and make an appointment with Mr. Jenkins.

He will give you Form 202 to fill out. Then you go to the fifth floor, third corridor on the left, turn right, go in the second door. You stand at the first desk and fill out Form 23-B, Requisition for Clothing Allowance. You take *that* to Building Three, room 508, third floor, second door, fourth desk and then—"

"Lord," Mom says, "By the time we get clothes for these chirren, they will have done outgrowed them."

"I don't make the rules," the lady says.

"Well, honey," says Mom, "I ain't got time to do all that, not right now. Tonight I got to go deliver a baby. Then I got to visit a sick old lady and work on her with some herbs. Then I got to go down to the courthouse and get a young man out of jail. He's not a bad boy, he's just been keepin' bad company. *Then* I got to preach a funeral."

The lady looked at Mom like she was seeing a spirit risen from the dead. "But you can't do those things!" she says.

But I happen to know Mom Luby *can*. She's a midwife and a herb doctor and an ordained minister of the Gospel, besides running a place to eat and drink after hours. And she wouldn't need Welfare for us if people would only pay her sometimes.

Mom says, "Honey, just come along and watch me." She picked up her old shopping bag full of herbs and stuff. Miss Rushmore picked up her case and followed like somebody in a trance. Mom has that effect on people sometimes.

They were gone about two hours, and me and Puddin' had a good time eating and joking and looking into everybody's card hands.

I was surprised to see Mom bring Miss Rushmore straight into the back room when they got back. She sat her down at the table and poured her a drink of corn. To tell the truth, that lady looked like she needed it. Her glasses was crooked, and her shoes were untied, and her hair had come loose from its pins. She looked kind of pretty, but lost.

"Mrs. Luby," she said after a swallow of corn, you don't need my help."

"Ain't it the truth," says Mom.

"I came here to help you solve your problems. But now I don't know where to begin."

"What problems?" Mom asks.

"You are raising these children in an unhealthy atmosphere. I am not even sure they are yours. And you are practicing law, medicine, and the ministry without a license. I simply can't understand it."

"Can't understand what, honey?"

The lady sighed. "How you got more done in two hours than I ever get done in two years."

"You folks oughta put me on the payroll," says Mom with a chuckle.

"We can't," says Miss Rushmore. "You're not qualified."

Lucas started laughing, and Bobo joined in, and then we all laughed, Mose and Zerline and Jake and Sissiemae and Puddin' and me. We laughed so hard we rocked the room and shook the house and laughed that social worker right out the door.

"She got a point though," Mom says after we finished laughing. "You need an education to fill out forty pieces of paper for one pair of shoes. Never you mind, chirren. We'll make out fine, like we always done. Cut the cards, Bobo. Walter, deal."

Guests in the Promised Land

Some people can't stand for anybody to be too nice to them. My friend Robert is like that. Give Robert a piece of candy and he'll look at it like it's poisoned, then hand it back to you. Invite him to your house, he'll look behind all the doors to see is somebody back there waiting to jump on him. Try and be his friend, he'll fight you every chance he gets. Cause he figures you really his enemy.

I used to wonder how Robert got that way, but then I figured as a race of people we're all suspicious, cause we scared of what the Man is going to pull next. If the Man *does* give us something, we think there's a catch to it. Most of the time we're right. But, right or not, we all got plenty of reasons to feel that way.

I just figure Robert got an extra dose, cause he's little, and popeyed, and bowlegged, and some ugly. And cause they ain't nothing else in his family but girls. Big bad-mouth girls who push him around and beat up on him. 'Sides which, one of Robert's shoulders is higher than the other, so he always looks like he left the coat hanger in his clothes.

How I got to be Robert's friend, and I mean his only friend, is by helping him do what he likes most in this world. Which is playing the piano. There ain't no room for a piano at his house, even if they had the money to buy one. There ain't even room for all the people, with all them sisters growing up and having babies. And Robert won't play at his church because it's full of girls and women. No guys go there except shaky old deacons and the fat rich preacher.

But my daddy tends bar, and in one corner of the bar where he works is a little stage with a piano. The bar ain't much, just a neighborhood hangout. It ain't had live entertainment in years. They just never bothered to get rid of the piano, is all. The piano ain't much either—it's old and beat-up and needs tuning. But Daddy lets Robert play it sometimes, and Robert loves it like it's a solid gold Steinway.

It would be nice if I could say Robert was another Les McCann or Erroll Garner. But the truth is all he can play is gospel music, and he don't play that very well. His mother and sisters drag him to church all the time, so gospel is the only music he knows. Old draggy hymns played with a slow funky beat.

Church music is OK if you like it, I guess. But I never spent much time in church, so I don't go for it much. Neither do most of the men who hang out in the bar, which is why Robert never gets to play very long. Somebody always turns on the jukebox and drowns him out with James Brown.

Robert would sleep in that piano if they let him. But my daddy only lets him play when the bar ain't too crowded.

Last summer the boss put in an air conditioner, so the bar *stayed* crowded. Robert hardly ever got a chance to play.

It was a dull summer all around. A man got shot by his wife; people got robbed; a couple of guys got stabbed. The usual ordinary things that go on on our block. But nothing much happened to us except our trip to the Cedarbrook Country Club. Everybody's sorry about the way it turned out, but it wasn't really Robert's fault.

Mr. Brown arranged the trip. Mr. Brown is a man who is always trying to improve conditions on the block. People keep telling him, forget it, it's no use. But he goes right on organizing block clubs and cleanup days and outings for kids. The next week the block is as dirty as ever and the kids are still going nowhere. But Mr. Brown keeps trying.

What he did was go to the Junior Chamber of Commerce to ask them for some outings for us. And the Jaycees, who are white businessmen, decided to let the kids visit their country clubs. Kids all over the city would have a day at a country club. A different club and a different day for each neighborhood.

Our club was Cedarbrook. And our day was July 19th.

None of us knew exactly what a country club was, but we were pretty excited. When the bus pulled up, Mr. Brown introduced us to the men who had invited us. He said, "This is Mr. So and So, and this is Mr. Such and Such." But they all asked us to call them Chuck and Buzz and Bud and Bill.

I never got the names straight because they all sounded alike. The men all looked alike too, with square jaws and thin lips and big horn-rim eyeglasses that hid their eyes. They all tried hard to be friendly. They tried so hard we all piled on the back of the bus and let them ride up front with Mr. Brown.

Most of us had never been out of the city before. As the bus rolled past houses with lawns a mile wide, I couldn't believe my eyes. We passed one house that had at least twenty rooms. I whispered, "That must be the country club."

"No, man," said Leroy, "that's somebody's house. My Mom works for people with a bigger house than that."

"Them whiteys got everything," said Jesse. "And you better believe they ain't givin' none of it away."

"They givin' us a day at this place, ain't they?" I asked.

"Shoot, that's just a loan," said Jesse, who is the baddest mouth on our block. "You they guest today. But you better be a *good* guest. Behave yourself and act grateful and don't take too much."

The bus rolled on through neighborhoods with hundreds of places that looked like movie stars' houses. And Jesse rapped on about always being guests and never owning nothing for ourselves. I guess if those guys up front had known how mad we were getting, they'd have called the whole thing off.

But they had no idea. The way we smiled when we got off the bus, you'd have thought we were a bunch of Moseses seeing the Promised Land.

That's what it was, all right. Only it didn't say nowhere it was promised to us. Not the lake, not the hills, not the lawns, not the trees, none of it.

"Welcome to Cedarbrook, fellows," said Buzz or Bud or Bill. "The place is yours. We want you to have a good time. If you'd like to play golf, go with Chuck here. Those who want to play tennis, go with Mike. If you want to swim, come with me."

The guys made a lot of phony excited noises and broke up into groups. I looked around for Robert. I was a little worried about him. He had been very quiet on the bus while Jesse and them were rapping. I had had a hard time talking him into the trip in the first place, and I had made up my mind to stay with him all day. But he'd vanished.

Then I I saw his raggedy old red shirt disappearing up the hill toward the clubhouse.

Mr. Brown saw it too. "Brunson!" he shouted at me. "Go get Shields and bring him back here!"

"Now, now, Mr. Brown," said Scoop or Chuck or Mike, "let the boys do what they want. I *said* the place was theirs."

He looked nervous, though. So did Mr. Brown. I think they had already decided the clubhouse would be off limits to us. But didn't neither of them stop me from following Robert.

I found him in what I guessed was the dining room. At

the door was a sign, GUESTS NOT ALLOWED WITHOUT MEM-
BERS. But I didn't need a sign to know we didn't belong in
that room, unless we were waiters or busboys. It had thick
carpets and mirrors and about forty tables covered with
cloths. A bar was along one wall. On the other wall was a
big, shiny grand piano. The kind that costs thousands of
dollars.

If it had been anybody else I would have said, "Come
on, let's get out of here."

But it was *Robert*, hiding his head behind his high shoulder, and rubbing his scruffy shoes together, and looking at
that piano with eyes big as teacups.

So I said, "Go on. They won't mind."

The only other person in the room was the bartender.
He looked at us kind of funny, but he didn't say anything.

"Go on," I said again.

So Robert sat down and started playing "Oh, Happy
Day." It wasn't bad, if you like church music. Of course
he hit a lot of wrong notes, but he made up for that with
feeling. He went on to "Joy of My Salvation" and "Jesus,
Lover of My Soul." By then, he was so wrapped up in the
music you couldn't have got him away from that piano if
a bomb had fallen on the place.

So I didn't bother to tell him that behind his back the
Jaycees and some other men were drifting into the room.
They got their drinks and stood at the bar, silently staring
at the little black boy at the big black piano.

Then Mr. Brown showed up, out of breath from running. What's-his-name, the one in charge, was with him.

So were Leroy and Jesse and the rest of the guys.

"Ahem," said What's-his-name.

Robert wouldn't stop playing.

"My friend," said What's-his-name, "wouldn't you rather be outdoors in the sunshine? There's a beautiful golf course out there."

But what does a kid like Robert, who's never even seen *grass*, know about a golf course?

I got the message, though. We weren't supposed to be in that room. Or anywhere in that building.

Mr. Brown got the message too. He grabbed Robert from behind and snatched his hands off the keys.

The men at the bar, who had been so quiet, suddenly came to life. "Give the kid a hand!" one cried. They all applauded and shouted things like "Bravo!" and "Wonderful!" as Robert got up from the piano.

Robert just stood there, his eyes darting around suspiciously. It doesn't pay to give him compliments, even if you mean it, because he doesn't believe you. But even *I* had a suspicion *these* cats weren't sincere.

There was a click, and a blade appeared in Robert's hand. Everyone gasped. I guess they thought he was going to use the knife on Mr. Brown or on What's-his-name.

What he did instead showed how really bad he was hurting. He turned and slashed a deep scar into that shiny piano. And another scar. And another.

"Why, you little *animal!*" cried What's-his-name. Mr. Brown got the knife away from Robert.

But that was the signal. All of us sort of exploded at once. We knew they didn't really want us there, and all those phony smiles and handshakes didn't mean a thing. Now it was out in the open. If Robert was an animal, we all were animals. We decided we might as well prove it.

No golf got played that day, but plenty of plates got smashed, windows got broken, and carpets got gashed and torn. I snatched down the GUESTS NOT ALLOWED sign and ripped it to pieces. By the time they called the security guards to herd us back on the bus, we must have done a thousand dollars' worth of damage.

The white men didn't ride back with us. Just Mr. Brown. He looked sad, hurt, and bewildered. Like he was thinking, How could you do this to me and those nice white men?

Robert looked sad too. But I knew what to say. "Don't worry, Robert," I whispered to him. "They won't invite us back again." Robert is a funny cat. He looked happier right away.

After a while we started singing "Oh Freedom" and "I'm on My Way" and other freedom songs. Robert joined in because they were hymns, and he knew them. I knew he'd never be quite so lonely again. I also knew we'd never go back there unless we could eat in the clubhouse and listen to him play, wrong notes and all.

Because it ain't no Promised Land at all if some people are always guests and others are always members.